STRIKE ZONE

. . . .

The Pro Book Three

RICHARD CURTIS

WOLFPACK PUBLISHING
— EST 2013 —

WOLFPACK PUBLISHING
— EST 2013 —

Strike Zone

Paperback Edition
Copyright © 2020 (As Revised) Richard Curtis

Wolfpack Publishing
6032 Wheat Penny Avenue
Las Vegas, NV 89122

wolfpackpublishing.com

Paperback ISBN 978-1-64734-965-3
eBook ISBN 978-1-64734-060-5
Library of Congress Control Number: 2020944855

STRIKE ZONE

. . . .

*For Dave Fisher—dear friend, splendid writer,
loyal client, and adequate outfielder*

Chapter I

· · · ·

I hereby make the following bona fide offer: if you can convince me that there is any single experience more satisfying than watching the first exhibition game of spring training, I will dispatch a check for one hundred smackers to your favorite charity. Yeah, yeah, I know what you're going to say. But believe it or not, given my choice between balling some Hollywood queen and sitting on a hard bleacher in Pompano Beach or St. Petersburg or Vero or Lauderdale or Tucson, my mind doesn't hesitate a fraction of a second.

Laugh if you will, but don't knock it if you haven't tried it.

By all rights today should have been no different. The early afternoon air over the St. Petersburg stadium was warm and dry and deliciously tangy with salt drifting in on a moderate Gulf breeze. I could feel my bones, all but frozen brittle by New York's bitterest winter in years, flexing restlessly in the sunbeams, tempting me to do something crazy like stripping and leaping onto the field and streaking to the center field wall. I was bathed in my favorite medium, spectators, and the best kind at that: pretty sports groupies, young and cow-eyed and enthusiastic, their firm, fair, peach-fuzzed limbs shooting out of shorts and tops so tight and skimpy I wondered why they bothered to dress at all.

And on top of all this, it was a good game, the New York Mets, St. Petersburg's "home" team, sitting on a 2-1 lead over the San Francisco Giants going into the seventh inning.

Had it been any other spring, I'd have been happier than a sow in a slop-trough. But not this spring. Not today. That old feeling was gone and I wondered if I'd ever get it back. And I wondered, too, how many other fans sitting here and in other exhibition parks across the South felt the same way and for that matter, how many of the players themselves? Was it my imagination, or was the atmosphere both on and off the field subdued, devoid of that zealous fervor spiced with zaniness that still makes baseball fans the greatest ones of all? After what had happened, could anyone ever again watch a baseball game with that innocent ardor of yore?

Maybe I was unduly sensitive to these gloomy thoughts because of the proximity of Willie Hesketh. He sat beside me in his wheelchair, both legs and arms in casts, watching the game with Spartan stolidity. He had scarcely moved or spoken since his wife, Alma, parked him on the ramp beside me in the third inning. I'd begged him not to come, for his sake as well as mine (to say nothing of poor suffering Alma), but some demonic, masochistic urge had driven him to insist. It was awful, horrible. I squirmed with anguish and guilt and fought back an impulse to flee. Every time there was a play to the Mets' left fielder, a rookie named Gene Pratt, I could feel the jealousy radiating out of Willie's soul like withering blasts of radioactivity. I knew that Willie was thinking, "That's my position, motherfucker. I should be fielding those balls. The fans should be cheering for me!"

In the top of the seventh, Pratt made a particularly fine play, a circus catch of a foul blooper near the stands, ending the inning. I automatically rose to my feet for the seventh inning stretch, then, remembering Willie, dropped remorsefully back to my seat. I looked sidelong at him and bit my lip. Moisture brimmed high in his dark eyes and began to flow down the creases of his walnut-colored cheeks and into his brushy black mustache. I wanted to die. I reached over and gripped his left hand, the hand they hadn't broken, and squeezed it to express the empathy I felt for him. But his flesh was cold and responseless, like a cadaver's. Nothing could penetrate the armor of pain Willie Hesketh wore today and unless he underwent a miracle of rehabilitation, he would wear it for the rest of his life. I wouldn't have blamed him if he were contemplating suicide at this moment, for his life as a ballplayer was over and for Willie life and ballplaying were synonymous. No one knew better than I what that meant. Hell, I'd almost committed suicide myself—suicide by inches, with alcohol—nine or ten years earlier after my football career with the Dallas Cowboys was shattered by an ankle-splintering tackle.

But the difference is that I'd suffered my injury honorably, in the line of duty. Willie had not. Willie had been beaten brutally in the vicious culmination of the most rancorous strike in sports history.

I squeezed his hand again, trying to make hope flow like electricity into his deadened flesh, to let him know that the heartache does eventually subside and you do eventually sweep the shards of broken dreams into the dustpan and build a new life for yourself as I'd done. But the agony was still too fresh and tender for Willie to comprehend this.

I can't tell you how relieved I was when he turned to me and said, "Dave, I think I'd like to leave."

"Whatever you say, Willie."

I looked up at Alma, whose beautiful oval face was contorted with ill-suppressed grief, and nodded. She kicked the brake on his wheelchair. Mine was only one of a dozen hands that offered to help but Willie waved everyone away.

And then, as Alma pivoted the chair and pushed it up the runway, an extraordinary thing happened. Billy Moffatt, the Giants pitcher, in the middle of his windup noticed Willie leaving. He stepped off the rubber, tucked the ball and his glove under one arm and began applauding Willie. For a moment the other Giants players looked bewildered. Then Roger Ainley at first base realized what was going on and he started applauding, too. Chris Speier at shortstop took it up, followed by Bobby Murcer, Gary Matthews, and Garry Maddox in the outfield. John Milner, the Mets first baseman at bat, stepped out of the batter's box and joined in. Mets started pouring out of the dugout, and I recognized Buddy Harrelson, Ed Kranepool, Randy Garrett, and Felix Millan among those joining in the accolade. In fact, the only Met not clapping was Gene Pratt, the kid who'd nailed down the job that undoubtedly would have been Willie's. I knew what he was thinking: as badly as he'd wanted that left field position, he didn't want to win his job that way.

Umpire Bill Cleavy took off his mask and saluted Willie with cap over heart. The fans rose out of their seats, in little clumps at first, then in waves, until not a soul remained seated as a cheer swelled from one side of the stadium to the other. Alma had turned the wheelchair around so Willie could see the ovation was for him. His eyes rounded with amazement and I could see his chin quivering with emotion. His fellow ballplayers had every reason to hate him, for, by declaring his intention to enter training camp while every other player in the major leagues was boy-cotting spring training, he had dealt a stunning blow to the strike, a blow which ultimately proved fatal to it. The players had scathingly reviled him. But Willie was to pay for his decision, pay for it with his pulverized limbs, pay for it with his career.

And yet, by extending him this ovation, the players were telling him they bore him no vindictiveness, that they under-stood how badly he had wanted to be a major league player, begin a great career with the Mets. And what's more, they were saying they not only forgave him but embraced him as one of their own. They deplored what had happened to him and recognized him for what he now was—a fallen ballplayer who still loved the game he would never play again.

Willie bowed his head in mute acknowledgment, then gestured brusquely for Alma to get him out of there before he broke down.

At that moment my mind flashed back to the first time I'd ever seen Willie. An old friend of mine coaching the Savannah Braves in the Southern League had called me to tell me about him. Willie had been burning up the league and a number of major league teams had received rave scouting reports on him. The Mets had begun negotiating with him to bring him up to New York in September to play out the last month of their losing season, just for a trial, and Willie had asked my friend what he should do. My friend had said, "Call Dave Bolt."

It had irked me to tear myself away from my office during one of the busiest seasons in the sports agent's year and I'd said to my friend, "This guy had better be worth it." As it turned out, Willie was gloriously, sublimely, exqui-sitely worth it. Watching him, I thought of another Willie I'd seen at the outset of a fabulous career when I was a kid.

Willie Hesketh had all of Willie Mays's strength, speed, and style, plus a certain finesse and intellectual grasp of strategy—what baseball people call "smarts"—that it took Mays several years of major league seasoning to refine.

I remembered, in particular, one circus catch he'd made on a sure home run to deep left center field, in which he had literally run up the wooden fence like a racing car climbing to the lip of a banked curve, snaring the ball and running down again. Later he told me he'd practiced that stunt dozens and dozens of times and it was really easier than it looked, except he was afraid one day he'd catch his spikes in the wood and leave his ankles up there.

I can't say his tryout with the Mets was a complete success but then I didn't expect it to be. He was nervous, disoriented, unfamiliar with his teammates and the opposition and was played in only eight or nine games. But he did hit eight for thirty at-bats, including a towering home run that I believe may still be rolling somewhere outside Shea Stadium and made some fielding plays that left no doubt in anyone's mind that Willie Hesketh was, barring injury, heading for superstardom. Barring injury: how bitterly that phrase stuck in my mind today.

I'd negotiated a nice but unspectacular bonus for him and a decent but unremarkable two-year contract. A few years earlier I might have gotten double or triple those sums but these were tight times. Most owners today prefer to pass up bonus babies with high price tags in favor of experienced players they can get in trades with other clubs. But I figured that if Willie coruscated in the major leagues as he'd done in the minors, maybe copping Rookie of the Year honors or something, he'd be able to write his own ticket when his contract expired. It's best not to be greedy—until you can get away with it.

Now all that was but a dream of the past, exploded, to use a famous line, like a raisin in the sun.

When I looked back to the playing field, it was blurred with my own tears. A violent wave of fury shuddered through me. I renewed my vow to find the men who'd destroyed Willie's career if it was the last thing I did on earth. . .

All winter long the air over the world of professional baseball had been acrid with dissension as negotiations over renewal of the contract between the owners and the Players Association broke down and finally broke off. There had been strikes in sports before, some more serious than others, but even as early as November, when the negotiators began their ritual of sparring and boasts to the press, you could see an ugly confrontation shaping up. There was none of the levity that usually attends the preliminaries, none of the easy confidence in a quick settlement, no sense of common ground, none of the extravagant demands made by cynical bargainers who expect to get only half of what they're asking. But Milton Blossom, director of labor relations for the owners, and Sam Metcalf, successor to Marvin Miller as head of the Players Association, had declared their positions with ominous, grim determination. When bargaining got under way in earnest after New Year's, it was clear that both groups meant what they said: they would not be budged.

Although that perennial favorite, the reserve clause, was a key issue, and some so-called freedom issues were on the agenda, too—freedom for players to dress, smoke, drink, and wench as they pleased on their own time—the nub of the conflict was, as always, money: higher starting salaries, bigger pensions, more medical benefits, bigger World Series shares, travel expenses, spring training allowances, dues checkoffs, and other fringe benefits. There was also a new demand, one that had been kicked around for years but never introduced seriously until now: the players wanted a percentage of every gate—a piece of the action, in other words.

Aside from the latter, all this was old news and the public at large figured things would be worked out in the tried and true give-and-take of the bargaining table, as had been done in previous years. But knowledgeable insiders knew differently; they knew there could be no give-and-take this time because there was nothing left to give and nothing left to take.

It had been coming for a long time. Professional sports had expanded violently in the last decade. Not just base-ball, but football, basketball, and hockey had swollen like dry sponges dropped in a pond. The leagues added new teams, new divisions, and new conferences. As if that wasn't enough, savvy promoters came along and added new leagues. And even that didn't seem to satisfy the gluttonous fans and the greedy promoters, so soon enterprising hus-tlers were pushing professional tennis, golf, boxing, soccer, horse-racing, auto-racing, dog-racing, jai-alai, lacrosse, team handball, roller derby, Canadian football, demolition derbies, frog-jumping contests, and marbles tournaments. And everyone behaved as if there were no tomorrow.

The salary wars unleashed in these go-go years stretched available funds precariously thin. Television networks were saturated with sports programming and were bitching louder and louder about how the hockey season ended almost two months after baseball season opened, and on any given weekend in early October, you could take your choice of a baseball game, a football game, a basketball game, or a hockey game on the boob-tube. Finally, they flatly refused to take on more sports programming for fear of viewer backlash. Nor was there any more money to be squeezed out of fans by raising ticket prices. Attendance had already dropped in all sports and even die-hard fans were vowing to boycott en masse—they'd actually formed an influential national lobby—if box office prices went up again.

These twin specters of overexpansion and overexposure had presided over the National Football League Players strike in 1974 and caused it to fizzle ridiculously. But this time they were joined by a third specter and there was nothing ridiculous about it, inflation. The monster had consumed everything baseball players had gained in their 1972 settlement, and more. Players making high five-digit salaries were barely treading water and those in the medium and lower range were actually suffering serious hardships, incredible as it sounded to the average sports-page reader.

So, the players had a legitimate grievance. But so did the owners and so did the networks and so did the fans. For the same ogre that was gobbling up the players' income was consuming everyone else's. The fact was, the cupboard was bare. But the players, still living in the dream world of a seller's market created in the recent years of plenty and unlimited growth, refused to believe it. And at length, they struck. . .

Like just about every other players' agent, I maintained a neutral stance during the developing conflict. Few people appreciate both viewpoints as keenly as agents, dealing as we do with both owners and players every day. In fact, I had even more insight into the problem than most of my colleagues, having been both a player and, later, a front office executive for the Dallas Cowboys before getting into agenting. Naturally, I was rooting for the players, if for no other reason than the selfish one that more money for them meant higher commissions for me. But it would have been imprudent for me to express this sentiment publicly, owners have long memories. Besides, I don't hold much by group actions of any sort—a throwback, I guess, to the frontier individualism of my forebears. I represent one player at a time, two at a time is a conspiracy, three is a political party, and four or more is communism. I'm just not a political animal. My daddy used to say, sooner wave your dick at a hungry bear than get involved in politics.

And so when, on a rainy Tuesday morning in the second week of March, about ten days after the strike had begun, I got a call from Grover Bailey, the Commissioner of Baseball, inviting me to lunch, I felt an emotion far from the flattery I'd have felt on some other occasion. He'd said nothing more than that he wanted to talk to me about the strike but that had been enough to slide a sharp dagger of apprehension into my guts. I not only didn't want to get involved, I didn't even want to be seen in the commissioner's presence at this critical time.

Even routinely, an agent constantly worries about getting the reputation of being a "management man," of siding with what players half-facetiously refer to as The Enemy. But now, with both sides digging trenches for a protracted and nasty quarrel, any fraternization with management (and say what you will, the Commissioner of Baseball represents management) could be misinterpreted by my clients and leave them with a lasting suspicion about where my sympathies lay. Luckily, Commissioner Bailey was sensitive enough to realize this and discreetly arranged for lunch not at his office or a public restaurant but in a private room at the University Club on West 54th Street.

The University Club may have been considered the apex of neo-classical style when it was built, but its gloomy, din-

gy baroqueness seemed better suited for exhibiting phara-
onic mummies than accommodating living members. The
foyer in which I stood waiting for the security man to pass
me through was an immense cube of smudged marbled
space surrounded by thick columns and furnished with
dismal green leather chairs and heavy tables. Overhead,
ornate filigree twined around dull frescoes almost illegible
with grime. I peered into a library the size of a tennis court,
through whose double windows facing Fifth Avenue the
cold light of rainy March scarcely illuminated the staid
men reading the Wall Street Journal or conferring in fune-
real whispers in a corner. I felt an insane desire to rip out a
fart—I don't mean a squeaker, but a big stentorian boomer
that would rattle the chandeliers. I suppressed the urge
and simply checked myself out in the large ormolu-framed
mirror on the south wall.

I sighed at the sight of myself. Unfortunately, I was
the same man who'd checked himself out in the mirror
on his closet door earlier that morning. One always hopes
that the angel who takes care of such things will one day
capriciously transform one's face into that of a Robert
Redford but I had to content myself this afternoon with the
same battered phiz I'd carried around for over thirty-five
years. No, check that, it had been a very nice phiz until I
started playing football, at which time my nose developed
a curious affinity for other people's elbows, knuckles, and
cleats. It had been set so many times it all but twitched
lasciviously whenever I passed a doctor's office. Recently it had gotten knocked off center again in a somewhat
belligerent exchange of views with a hockey player who
thought I was making it with his wife. It made a clicking
sound when I wiggled the cartilage with my fingers but it
had a great natural ridge for supporting sunglasses.

This unfortunate organ was the centerpiece of an otherwise pleasant face. My eyes are blue and generate a vacuous expression most of the time. This is a matter of policy, to make people think I'm a little slow on the uptake. It's always a good idea to make people underestimate you. Among the nicknames I've had—and "Bolt" is a magnet for nicknames—is "Sleeper," because I lulled opposing football players into thinking I had lead in my pants, then burned them with my 9.4 speed or turned them around with my fancy moves.

Topping this face is a carpet of tightly kinked blond hair which, I'm ninety percent certain, comes about because an ancestor of mine seduced a slave girl and claimed the issue as his own son, don't ask me why. This means I'm a tiny part Negro which shouldn't make a difference. But when you're a Southerner, where a tiny part Negro makes you a hundred percent nigger, it plays an enormous part in fashioning your attitudes. Happily, for me at least, the attitudes it has fashioned are the kind I'm proud of, a sensitivity to and feeling of kinship with minority people, certainly no disadvantage when you're as intimately involved with athletes as I am.

Anyway, the rest of the package is a six-foot-three frame supporting one hundred ninety-five well-conditioned pounds draped in quiet but expensive slacks, open-collared sports shirt, and blazer. Except for the hair, the man in the mirror was of a type you can see in the box seats of any sporting event in the country.

The security guard hung up the phone and directed me to a bank of elevators on the west wall of the club, past the coat-check room where two bored boys in uniform watched me with arrogant eyes. I ascended to the seventh floor, stepped out onto a worn red carpet and turned left until I found a door numbered 6. I tapped on it with one knuckle and pushed it open when I heard a muffled invitation.

I entered a large paneled room hung with nineteenth-century fox-hunting engravings. In the middle of the room stood a round dinner table set with two places in sparkling Spode, crystal, and sterling. Against one wall was a magnificent Regency sideboard waxed to a fare-thee-well and beside it, a low cocktail table with four leather chairs. In one of these sat Grover Bailey, the Commissioner of Baseball.

He was drinking a Manhattan and reading the latest issue of Sports Illustrated. From the glower on his face, I intuited he was scanning Dan Jenkins's caustic article on the strike. Without looking up, he said, "You still take bourbon and branch water, don't you, Dave?"

"Good memory, Commissioner."

A glossy-haired, tuxedo-clad man whom I hadn't noticed behind me flashed across the room to a fully stocked liquor caddy and a moment later, offered me my drink on a little silver tray. I stood, waiting for Bailey to finish the article. I knew he wasn't being rude. Rather, he was totally absorbed and, from what I could gather, not a little ticked off. I'd have thought that by now the commissioner would have grown a hide impervious to criticism but Jenkins had really keelhauled him in the article, laying the blame squarely on his shoulders for not jawboning both sides into coming to terms. Bailey's predecessor, Bowie Kuhn, by consensus an ineffective administrator, would have rolled with Jenkins's punch, but Bailey prided himself in being a strong man, if not exactly a czar, and the charge of passiveness must have stung him bad.

He slapped the magazine shut and dropped it heavily on the table, emptied the rest of his drink down his throat and signaled the waiter for a refill as he rose to shake my hand. "Now I know how Abraham Lincoln felt," he sighed, gesturing at the magazine.

I was tempted to extend the metaphor with a joke about freeing the slaves—"slavery" being the current pet propaganda word of the striking ballplayer—but thought better of it after a glance at his stern and humorless eyes. The commissioner was in no mood for jocularity.

Our waiter returned with the commissioner's drink and we settled into the leather chairs, which made long whistles as the air squeezed through seams in the upholstery. Bailey's cushion had a higher pitch than mine because he was heavier by perhaps fifty pounds. Not plump, exactly, because he was a tall and big-boned man, but from the way his stomach bulged over his trousers when he was in a seated position I could see that his muscles found it difficult to contain his bulk as they must have once. He had a square face with thin, sandy hair, a prominent nose, a wide mouth canopied by a fuzzy red mustache, and intelligent eyes. Formerly a captain of industry—I think he made a fortune in real estate—then owner of a short-lived and ill-fated National League expansion club, the Charleston Privateers (now in its third incarnation in Tucson), he'd been the compromise choice of the owners when Kuhn stepped down. Then he'd double-crossed them by showing surprising forcefulness and innovation when he took office. I felt deeply sorry for him that he'd gotten so embroiled in this conflict before he'd built up enough clout to force both sides to resolve their differences. Given a little more time, he might have been a Pete Rozelle.

"I know you've done your best, Commissioner," I said.

We toyed with our drinks for a moment, then Bailey darted a look at the hovering presence of our waiter. "That'll be all for now, Eddie," he commanded. "I'll call you when we're ready to order."

"Very good, Mr. Bailey," Eddie said with a Scottish burr, disappearing through a door that presumably led to the kitchen.

"Well, Dave, how's business?"

How my business was was scarcely the purpose of this meeting but whatever the purpose was, the commissioner was obviously averse to pouncing into it. I'd have to follow his scenario. "Better than ever, Commissioner. My client list seems to be doubling every year without my trying too hard. Of course, my overhead is doubling, too, but all in all, I can't complain."

"You get a lot of referrals."

"I guess I have a lot of satisfied customers. I started with a handful of football players a few years ago. Now I've got a gross of athletes."

He smiled. "Is that how you measure them, by the gross?"

"Some of my colleagues measure them by the pound, like meat on the hoof."

"I sometimes think..." He censored the thought and sipped his drink. "What do you think of the latest developments?"

"Which ones do you mean? Last time I heard, negotiations had broken down completely."

"I thought you'd heard. The owners announced today they are seriously considering canceling the season. Blossom's statement'll be in the Post this afternoon."

"Cancel the season," I sneered. "That'll be the day."

"Don't be so sure. They're in a very rank mood. Their backs are to the wall."

"But half of them would be ruined!"

"Never underestimate an owner's capacity for writing off losses. I sometimes think half these guys pray for losses, to offset the windfalls they make in their other businesses."

"I can't believe they're serious."

"Take it from me, they are. Sure, they'll lose money, a lot of money. And some of them will go under. But do you see what their strategy is?"

"Sure. It would be a decisive way of breaking the strength of the Players Association, maybe permanently."

"Exactly. The owners take a beating this year but they're in the driver's seat forever after."

"The government would step in long before that happened."

"That's open to debate, Dave. Remember, baseball is the only professional sport not subject to federal antitrust statutes. The 1922 Supreme Court decision, reinforced by Toolson vs. New York Yankees in 1953 and the rejection of Curt Flood's suit a couple of years ago—hell, I don't have to run it down for you. But what they amount to, in a word, is that professional baseball is still technically a local sport and the federal government doesn't have a law on its books that would sanction intervention."

I took a long tug on my drink. "That's pretty heavy."

"Very heavy, my friend, very heavy indeed."

What about arbitration?"

"Oh, we tried arbitration at an early stage. We brought in Lew Hillsdorf, who settled that garment workers' strike last winter. After two days he walked out and do you know what he said to me? He said, 'They can both go fuck themselves.'" Bailey smiled for the first time.

"And a cooling-off period, what about that?"

"The players are against it. They remembered what happened in '74 in the NFL strike. The owners used the cooling-off period to break the strike. The baseball players won't get sucked into the same trap."

I finished my drink and went to the bar to fix myself another. "Christ, what ever happened to the simple days when baseball was just a game?"

"It never was just a game if you know your history. The reserve clause was created in 1879 and baseball has been a business ever since."

I sat down heavily again. "You said 'developments', in the plural. What's the other development?"

"The other is that the Players Association has signed a secret agreement with a nationwide labor union."

"What?" I almost spilled my drink.

"I found out about it last night. Sam Metcalf has been talking for weeks to two unions, the Federation of Skilled Workers and the United Craftsmen's Brotherhood. One of my... er... informants, has kept me abreast and reported that Metcalf had finalized a pact with Pinky Ryan of the FSW."

"What kind of pact?"

"Oh, what they call 'mutual interest.'"

"Meaning what, in plain English?"

"Meaning the possibility of sympathy strikes. Some of the other unions in Ryan's federation—he has skilled workers in steel, construction, and a few other important areas—could walk off the job in sympathy with baseball players."

"And vice versa!"

"And vice versa. Can you picture it, Dave? Baseball players sitting down mid-season because a bunch of riveters somewhere aren't getting a half-hour coffee break every morning?"

"I can picture it, I can picture it! But I'm still not convinced it's more than a gambit. Remember when there was talk a couple of years ago about athletes linking up with the Teamsters? That went nowhere fast."

"Yes, but largely because club owners fell in with the athletes' demands. Players in every professional sport have made fantastic gains in the last decade, so they haven't had to resort to outside muscle. This time, it's a different story. A very different story." He closed his eyes a moment and shuddered. "Shall we order lunch?"

Lunch was a slab of roast beef as thick as a dictionary and softer than wet tissue, borne over the gullet on a stream of robust Mouton Cadet bottled, in Bailey's phrase, when Ford Frick was commissioner. The conversation became general and chatty and Bailey avoided the subject of the strike by miles, like the leader of an expedition skirting a malarial swamp. Yet I had a feeling that by ignoring it altogether, he was foisting it on my attention, compelling me to wonder where, in this welter of gossip and anecdotes and locker-room jokes, was the point of this meeting.

I also had a sense of being weighed and measured, as if for some special task. But as I couldn't fathom what that might be, I just went along, quipping and yarning and pretending I lunched with the commissioner every day of the week. Bailey's eyes expressed nothing but cordiality but I knew he was gathering and filtering impressions and molding them into an opinion. I was molding an opinion of my own: that this was a very, very shrewd man.

Dessert (rum-laced mousse), coffee (espresso), wine (a silky port), brandy (Armagnac), and cigar (Cuban), and I was climbing the wall with curiosity.

Then it came, softly and subtly, like a leaf of notepaper drifting to the ground.

About a quarter of the way down his cigar, Bailey cleared his throat and said, "We talked about referrals before."

"Yes?"

"I was referred to you, too."

I looked at him blankly. "Beg your pardon?"

"I've been told," he said, "that you can get a certain kind of job done."

I looked at him steadily, hoping I didn't look as fatuous as I felt but I really had to confess I didn't have clue one as to what he was talking about.

"I'm referring to jobs you did for Niles Lauritzen and Vincent Sturdevant."

"Ah."

The clouds began to part. Niles Lauritzen and Vincent Sturdevant were, respectively, commissioner of the American Basketball Association and president of the National Hockey League. The "certain kind of job" Bailey alluded to referred to a couple of—for want of a better phrase—undercover detective assignments I'd undertaken for them. It had all started when a client I'd just signed, basketball leviathan Richie Sadler, was abducted and I had to find him and bring him back before it hit the headlines. I did it, too, though at considerable cost: my face, nuts, and other choice parts had to go into drydock for refitting.

And then when, some time later, the National Hockey League required somebody to keep the lid on a gambling scandal that threatened to befoul the sacred name of professional hockey, Niles Lauritzen had commended me to Vincent Sturdevant as a skillful, discreet operative. The fact that I accomplished that mission, too—though not, once again, without taking some hard knocks—apparently enhanced my reputation. And now, with Commissioner Bailey hinting at some similar assignment, I realized that what had started, for me, as an extracurricular activity was rapidly becoming a semi-official function. Need a trouble-shooter? Can't go to your regulars? Bring in Dave Bolt.

There is substantial doubt in my mind as to the accuracy of the adjectives "skillful" and "discreet" applied to my handling of those two situations. Looking back at them, I see a bumbling amateur playing Junior G-Man in a very high-stake game, using his instincts, a little cleverness and fast-talk, one or two head-fakes and a whole lot of trial-and-error groping, and succeeding more in spite of than because of himself. Aspiring private eyes seeking lessons in how not to solve crimes would find it most rewarding to study my procedures if they're even worthy of that term. I made every mistake in the books, got myself thrashed resoundingly on several occasions and prevailed only because luck was smiling on me that day. But I suppose that Commissioner Bailey, like every other executive in the wonderful world of sports, had read no further than the bottom line where it said He Got The Job Done and that was good enough for him.

The clouds had begun to part, although I was still in the dark about what he was getting at. But I felt another surge of anxiety coming on. An instinct told me I was not going to like what he said and not just because I don't particularly enjoy these secret service gigs. Enjoy them or not, I do them out of a combination of duty, love of professional sports and the people who populate them, and money. But if Bailey's proposition had to do with the strike—and what else could it have to do with?—it was hard for me to conceive a way of going along with it without ending up on either the owners' shitlist, the players', or both.

So, in the moment following Bailey's statement, I hastily erected a fortress of objections, excuses, and demurrers against anything he might ask me to do. When the last stone was in place, I finally said, "What seems to be the problem, Commissioner?"

He tamped a fine white ash into the marble ashtray on the cocktail table. "I'm deeply concerned about this linkup between the Players Association and the Federation of Skilled Workers. No, not just for the reasons we discussed before—though God knows those are sufficient. What concerns me is that the FSW may be infiltrated by criminal elements."

I nodded thoughtfully. "You have evidence?"

"No, nothing concrete. Just some rumors based on certain incidents."

"What kind of incidents?"

"Oh, you know, the usual things one can expect from an aggressive young union organizing shops and treading on the toes of management, workers, other unions."

"You mean, strong-arm tactics, sabotage, like that?"

"Yes."

"And you want concrete evidence?"

He nodded. "If the FSW is subject to underworld influence, a coalition with the Players Association could be disastrous. The mob would have a hook right up professional baseball's giggy where we'd never be able to pull it out. The leverage they could assert—well, it's frightening to contemplate." As if to emphasize the frightful nature of his contemplation, he tossed an inch of Armagnac down his throat. You just don't do that to Armagnac.

"So what you want me to do is get the goods on this union," I said.

"If there are goods to get. Let me make my position perfectly clear, to use a well-worn phrase. I am opposed to any alignment between the players and any union other than their own Association. However, I would not intercede if the rank-and-file of ballplayers voted ultimately in favor of such an alignment, unless—unless there was evidence of criminal involvement in that union. Then I not only would intercede, I would fight it with every ounce of energy I have. So I'm keeping an open mind until I have all my information. And I want you to gather that information for me. How you do it is your business. I'll, of course, place the complete financial and manpower resources of my office at your disposal." He dropped his hands limply into his lap as if the effort of coming out with the proposition had exhausted him.

I was slumped in my chair gazing bemusedly at the ceiling and I hoped I gave Bailey the impression of giving his proposition the most serious consideration. Actually, I'd already made up my mind to reject it.

"I would not, you know, expect you to do this for free," Bailey said, making sure I was weighing all factors on my scale. "In fact—"

I cut him off with a wave of the hand, feeling a little embarrassed. I knew he'd be generous; there was no need to put him in the position of supplicant. "Tell me, Commissioner, why me? I know you have your own security staff."

"That's just it. Dave, whether you believe it or not, I'm trying to build an image of bipartisanship for my administration. I want the players to feel I'm as much for them as I am for their bosses. If I haven't acted more forcefully up to now—and this is something Dan Jenkins failed to understand," he interjected, toeing the Sports Illustrated on the table like a hideous insect, "it's because I'm desperately eager to shake off the reputation this office has for being a branch of management. Do you see what I'm getting at? An official investigation of the Federation would be interpreted as an attempt to smear the Players Association and break the strike. Whereas if it were undertaken by you. . ." He grappled for words. "You are one of the few people in professional sports who have the unequivocal respect of both sides. You're a fair man, a straight-shooter."

I sighed. "Yes, Commissioner. And that's precisely why I have to turn your offer down."

He blinked and seemed to have difficulty catching his breath.

"What do you suppose," I said, "would happen to my own reputation for bipartisanship if my investigation was responsible for breaking the players' strike?"

He pounded his palm with his fist. "But Dave, my aim is not to break the strike. It's to keep this sport clean and above reproach."

"You know that and I know that. But we also know that the same hotheads among the strikers who would accuse you of being a stalking-horse for the owners would accuse me. And I don't have to tell you what happens to an agent who comes to be known as a stalking-horse for the owners."

"I don't think that would happen," he said halfhearted-ly. The fact that that was the strongest argument he could muster was damning proof of his own serious doubts. He recognized this himself, exhaling languorously. "Oh well, it was worth a try."

"I'm really sorry, Commissioner. The last thing I want to do is add to your burden."

He looked at me tiredly and got to his feet with another heavy expiration of breath. "My burden," he muttered. Then he rallied with a smile. "If you weren't a goddam Reb, you'd have more sympathy for the Abe Lincolns of this world."

I raised both hands. "This is one civil war I'm staying neutral for, Commissioner."

"You can try but civil wars suck everybody into them sooner or later," the history buff reminded me.

I laughed. But within a week that remark would come back to bite me.

Chapter II

• • • •

It was still raining when I stepped out of the University Club. The blustery March wind penetrated my sheepskin-lined raincoat and drove pellets of sleet down my neck. I waited in vain for a taxi on Fifth Avenue. Hating over-heated buses on inclement days, I finally tramped back to my office on 42nd Street twelve blocks south wondering why I had this machismo thing against wearing hats and carrying umbrellas when it rained. The walk also gave me a chance to think again about the commissioner's proposal and I concluded I'd done the right thing. Bailey would not be overly pleased with me but if he was a fair man, he could not help but respect my decision.

I stepped into the lobby of the Lincoln Building across 42nd Street from Grand Central Terminal, shook myself like a wet dog, and took the elevator up to the eighteenth floor. I felt a tingle of pride as I paused outside the twin doors gilt-lettered "Suite 1810-1812," beneath which glittered "Red Dog Players Management Agency." It had started as merely "Room 1810" some four years back when it was just me and my secretary Trish in two claustrophobic cubicles the size of walk-in closets. My client list consisted of three over-the-hill running backs, a rookie pitcher for the St. Louis Cardinals, a basketball forward with knees torn up a little worse than Sixth Avenue, and a hockey defenseman so bad they'd nicknamed him Swish.

But we'd worked our asses off and slowly picked up new clients, good clients. And they'd talked to other players who eventually became clients. A few breaks, a few big-name stars, a few notable deals, and a lot of word-of-mouth, and the agency came of age. We'd expanded recently, leasing the adjoining offices and busting down the walls between them to create a spacious complex consisting of an attractive reception area, my own large office overlooking Grand Central Terminal, offices for Trish and my other assistant, Dennis Whittie, a conference room, a storage room, a utility room where my Xerox copier shared space with a coffee urn, water cooler, and Pitney-Bowes stamp machine, and finally, to Trish's everlasting gratitude, a john of our own instead of the inconvenient convenience down the hall. Trish had engaged a twittering brace of faggots to decorate the place and though they and I didn't exactly see eye to eye on the definition of the word "virile," they had imbued the suite with something approximating a masculine texture and at least rescued it from some vulgar excesses I'd been pushing for.

I opened the door and felt the same slight shock I always experienced upon finding the secretary-receptionist's seat filled by someone other than Trish. The previous year she'd staged a palace revolution, demanding greater responsibilities and I'd conferred some on her. She'd handled them so well I'd promoted her to full-fledged assistant and replaced the secretarial vacuum with a pretty brunette creature named Gillian Partridge, an English import with a lilting accent and a flair for drudgery, a perfect amanuensis in all respects but one: she didn't know diddly about sports. Like so many other American bosses, I'd fallen for that accent and only after the charm of it had worn off did I realize that Gillian was a staggering liability. I shuddered every time she had to make small talk with a client. She'd say things like, "Ah, you're a tackle. In which sport, exactly?" And yet, most of my clients found her intoxicating—that accent again and Gillian's enchanting naiveté. So I never quite got around to canning Gillian.

Oh yes, one more reason why I kept her; she hadn't the faintest interest in balling me. This may sound strange until you consider that Trish had pursued this goal with fanatical dedication for years, tantalizing me with her pert body and saucy ways and electrifying innuendoes, constantly challenging my scruples about messing around with office help. I'd successfully managed to evade her grasp all this time by reminding myself that a great secretary in the hand is worth two bed-partners in the bush.

I looked past Gillian's desk and watched Trish hammering out some scheme or another on the phone. Gone was that joyous insouciance, those shocking miniskirts and see-through bra-less tops, those pouting lips and flicking tongue. In their place, the erect posture of a busy executive, clad in demure, tailored, unrevealing tweed. My promotion of her had put a stop to the fun and games. She no longer wanted to ball me.

All she wanted to do now was marry me.

"Here are your messages, Mr. Bolt," Gillian said, sliding a little handful of pink slips across her desk. I grabbed them and slouched into my office, feeling slightly out of temper. Arriving in the big time has its drawbacks as well as its assets. Some fun goes out of your life. As I'd just told Commissioner Bailey, you double your client list, you double your overhead as well, and that included the overhead of having to take life more seriously.

The messages Gillian gave me formed a cross-section of a sports agent's life: a hockey star asking me if it was all right to address a Kiwanis luncheon without charging a fee (absolutely not); a toy company asking permission to use the likeness of one of my clients on a new quarterback doll (sure, for a royalty on every doll sold); a basketball player hitting me up for another advance (I really should charge interest—I have more money out on the street than the Mafia); a slacks manufacturer seeking an endorsement by one of my golfer clients (by now, you can guess what my answer was); and Willie Hesketh. . . well, I didn't know just what Willie might be calling about.

I wondered if it had anything to do with the strike. Strikes hurt everybody but rookies have the most to lose. If they join the strikers, they put themselves at once on the bad side of the manager or owner. If they don't join the strikers, they earn the enmity of their teammates, which can prove equally fatal to an aspirant.

I called Willie in Astoria, Queens, where he and Alma rented a little apartment not too far from Shea Stadium.

"What's up, Willie?"

"Oh, it's about this strike thing. I've come to a decision and Alma and I want to come in and talk to you about it."

"A decision? What is there to decide?" I said.

"Are you free for a drink after work today?"

"Today? That sounds urgent."

"It kinda is."

I shrugged. "Come on in. Meet me at the Bull and Bear. That's in the Waldorf Astoria. Six o'clock okay?"

"Sure."

There really is no "after work" for an agent. Crises come up around the clock, or at least, what my clients consider crises: fights with their wives, lost good luck charms, snoring roommates, a dose of clap. You name it, I've been woken up at three with a phone call about it. Another thing is, a lot of an agent's dealings are with the West Coast which is three hours behind New York time. But for the sake of argument, an agent's work as commonly defined begins to slope off around 5:30. I conferred hastily with Trish and Dennis about some minor problems, then walked over to the Bull and Bear. It had stopped raining and the air had warmed a few degrees, presenting an intoxicating promise of spring.

Willie and Alma sat, or one might say huddled, in a corner booth. Willie was an impressive, square figure in a white turtleneck sweater and plum-colored blazer, Alma a tiny slip of a thing with glossy black hair flowing like a raven's feathers out of a floppy maroon beret. They looked around furtively, Willie checking out the booth behind them to see if it was occupied by someone he didn't want to see. Very odd.

We pressed flesh and ordered drinks. Willie reached into his jacket pocket and took out a pack of Marlboros, lighting one apologetically.

"Tut, tut," I said.

He shrugged. "Don't worry, chief. When the season begins—if it begins—I'll quit. Right now, I need to smoke."

"Okay, but I figure every puff is worth about a buck to me in lost commissions. Smoking cuts down your longevity, you know."

Under his brushy mustache, Willie's white teeth bared in a grin as he dragged deeply on the cigarette, opened his wallet, and tossed a dollar at me while exhaling in my face. Alma shook her head in mock disapproval.

"What's up, Willie? You said something about the strike."

He leaned forward confidentially. "Dave, it's got me real uptight."

"It's got everybody uptight, son."

"Yeah, but. . ." The drinks arrived and Willie clutched his glass as if it were a hanger strap on a lurching subway train. Then he drew another big lungful of smoke. "See, I've been thinking. . . I mean, Alma and me's been talking. . . well. . ."

"Spit it out, Willie."

"Okay. How would it be if I went to training camp?"

"When?"

"Now."

"Now? You mean, during the strike? You mean, you reckon to cross the picket line?"

"Uh-huh."

I tapped the table. "I was afraid it might be something like that."

"In other words, you don't approve."

"It's not a question of approval, Willie. A decision like that is strictly a matter between you and your conscience."

Alma laughed. "You his conscience, man—we pay you ten percent to be his conscience."

I patted her hand and looked back at Willie. "Buddy, I'll stand by you whatever you do. But I want to make sure you've thought it all out."

"He's done nothing but think for the last week," Alma said. "Heck, he been moping around the house like a puppy that had an accident."

"I've turned it over and over in my mind," Willie said.

"I'm sure. But you know, this strike is the most serious in memory. I've never seen the sides so far apart. Neither group has broken ranks. Not one owner has made a concil-iatory gesture. Not one player has crossed the picket line. Now, the first one who does—well, he's going to be like

the cow who tested the quicksand. I'd be genuinely worried for that man's safety. This is a very rough situation,
Willie, rougher in fact than most people know, take my
word for it." I couldn't tell him about my meeting with the
commissioner, but I tried to convey in my troubled gaze
the special knowledge Bailey had imparted to me.

His eyes acknowledged the message and he pursed his
lips. But I could see that while I'd made his decision harder, I hadn't affected it materially. He took a deep breath
and spoke with new confidence in his voice. "Dave, like
the saying goes, I came to play baseball. I'm pretty certain
I can nail down a starting spot, but with every day of this
strike that goes by, the odds against me go up. You know
how conservative managers are. When training camp finally opens up, there'll be little time for rookies to prove
themselves. The team's gonna go with the man who held
the job the year before. Who knows how long it'd be before
I got another chance?"

"You've got to give managers a little more credit than
that," I said. "Strike or no strike, they're still looking to
put together the best team they can. They're going to give
everybody a chance to win a starting slot."

"Yes, but opening day is only three weeks away."

"Maybe so, but who are you going to play with after
you cross the picket line? Yourself? You'll be the only
one out there. You'll be the only one playing in the major
goddam leagues!"

"The coaches'll work with me," he said. "And when the
rosters are drawn up, they'll remember me. I suppose that
sounds contemptible, like I'm bucking for brownie points. . ."

"It will seem like that to a lot of people," I answered.

He took a long swallow of his drink, then brought his
glass down on the table with a startling crack. "Goddam-

mit, Dave, I don't give a shit what it sounds like. This is my career we're talking about, my life! I may never get another chance like this again."

"There's plenty of chances for a player of your caliber."

"That's easy for you to say but I've never left things to chance. The way I grew up, if you saw an opportunity to get the jump on the next guy, you took it. If the other players want to call me scab or chicken shit or brown nose or anything else, that's cool with me. The only thing I care about is being called the starting left fielder for the New York Mets."

I finished my drink. "Sounds to me like you've made up your mind."

"I kind of have. I just wanted to know if. . . if you'll back me up."

I looked at Alma. "What do you say?"

"I'm worried but I'll stand by him."

"You may get some phone calls, people calling your husband a lot of disagreeable names."

"I can deal with that," she said.

Willie tilted his head. "What do you say, chief? Do I have your blessing?"

I covered his big leathery hand with my own. "You got it, Willie."

I reached for my wallet but he raised his palm and drew his own billfold out of his jacket. "This one's on me, chief."

I walked them through the warm mist to the subway station at Lexington Avenue and 53rd Street. It was dark; the approaching spring had not noticeably lightened the sky at this hour and the realization that winter was still with me weighed depressingly on my shoulders. I locked hands alternately with Alma and Willie, then watched them trot down the subway stairs. Something prompted me to shout, "Willie, be careful, for crying out loud."

They paused on the landing and Willie saluted me. "Right you are, chief."

And that was the last time I saw him in one healthy piece.

From subsequent talks with Willie and other people involved in the incident, I've managed to put together a reasonable re-creation of what next happened.

When he got home, he called Ralph Luckinbill, general manager of the New York Mets and told him about his decision to drive down to St. Petersburg and report to training camp. Needless to say, Luckinbill almost fell off his chair for joy and promised unimpeded passage through the picket line when Willie arrived. Luckinbill asked if he could announce the news to the press. At that point Willie should have called me; I'd have told him to wait till he got down there before making the announcement. And to the extent that I failed to consider this point when we were discussing the situation over drinks that night, I must hold myself responsible for what happened. Anyway, Willie told Luckinbill sure, why not send out a release now—it was going to hit the news sooner or later anyway. So, that night the release went out and the story appeared side by side with that of the owners' threat to cancel the baseball season. The Heskeths' humble little house in Astoria was inundated with reporters the next morning as Willie loaded his Dodge Dart for the three-day trip south and his actual departure was attended with slightly more ceremony than the launching of a Cunard flagship.

The ubiquity of the press in the following days played a key part in what finally happened, for Willie's progress was covered as closely as a presidential motorcade. Declaring that Willie's arrival in St. Petersburg would trigger a bloody confrontation with the players picketing spring training camp there, reporters from a hundred different papers, press services, and radio and television networks traced his movement south from day to day, charting him like a comet on a collision course with a planet. Try as he might to keep a low profile, apparently, half the motel owners on the Eastern Seaboard were on the lookout for him in hope of being able to boast he'd patronized their establishments. Thus on each of the roughly four-hundred-mile legs of his journey, his whereabouts quickly became known soon after he checked in for the night.

He spent his first night outside of Durham, North Carolina, and the second in Waycross, Georgia. The following morning he set out early for his final destination, St. Petersburg, amidst a clamor of reporters and cameramen. He drove for a little over an hour, had breakfast in Wilcox, Florida, and had just resumed his journey when he picked up a pair of headlights in his rear-view mirror. It was only a little after seven in the morning and the first light of dawn was obscured by a lowering cloud cover. It was drizzling. Thus Willie could make out no detail of the car behind him but was fairly sure it was deliberately trailing him. However, it didn't concern him very much, because he figured it was some newshound trying to scoop his colleagues.

But as he rounded a bend south of Wilcox, the pursuing car sped up and overtook him, edging him onto the shoulder. Willie peered into the dim gap between cars and made out at least two men in the front seat and two in the back and the one in the passenger's seat in front was waving for him to pull over. Willie cursed and glided to a halt in the emergency lane. He got out and began walking up to the car behind, shouting at these jokers to fuck off. It did not cross his mind that they could be anyone else but press people.

All four doors of the car opened at once and Willie, to his horror, saw baseball bats in the hands of the black-clad men who poured out. He pivoted and raced back to his car, dove back into the front seat and punched the locks on the front and rear doors on the driver's side. Then he lunged for the locks on the other. But he didn't move fast enough. One of the men yanked open the front door on the passenger side, grabbed Willie's arm and hauled him out of the car.

Willie had grown up in the South Chicago ghetto and learned at an early age that there was no such thing as a fair fight. He brought his free fist up with all his might into the man's testicles and heard a satisfying yowl of agony. The man released him but by then the other three figures were grappling with him. He flailed wildly, cuffing all of them but getting none of them decisively. A bat struck him a glancing blow on his shoulder and another a solid pummel on the ribs. He knew it was a lost cause but he was determined to take somebody with him. His fingers found the hair on a head and with his other hand he raked the man's face with his fingernails. The last thing Willie remembered clearly was thrusting a finger into the guy's eye and feeling the gush of fluid as his finger sank deep into the socket. Then a hard, dull pain shattered his skull. In his rapidly fading consciousness, he was aware of other blows on his back and arms and head, and off in the distant darkness someone was screaming, "My eye! My eye! My eye. . .!"

About an hour later, a passing motorist found Willie's Dart resting on its side at the bottom of an embankment. Willie lay crumpled in the driver's seat, his face painted with viscid blood like some ghastly totem, his right arm crooked in a hideously unnatural angle, the bloody fingers of his right hand splayed in four different directions like signpost arrows at a crossroad.

The Florida State Police were summoned and a medical unit from the nearby town of Nantes. A Sergeant Krebs was the first man to reach the scene and as soon as he discovered the identity of the victim, he grasped the significance of the situation and called the Mets' offices in St. Petersburg. Mickey Snelling, the Mets' press liaison, after practically passing out from the shock of Krebs's news, finally recovered his cool and secured the policeman's assurance that no word would be given to the press until an official story could be prepared. Then Mickey and three other front-office executives chartered a helicopter and arrived at Nantes General Hospital a little over an hour later.

I was lunching at Manny Wolf's with Fred Shero, coach of the Philadelphia Flyers, when the headwaiter discreetly whispered into my ear that I had an urgent phone call. I excused myself and took the call on the phone at the maître d's reservation desk. A woman's voice said, "Please hold for Commissioner Bailey," and I felt a thunderbolt of apprehension in my chest. For if Bailey had gone to the trouble of tracing me and interrupting my lunch, it had to be a matter of tremendous urgency.

"Dave, an awful thing has happened," he blurted in a voice quavering with fright and grief. "Willie Hesketh has had an accident."

I felt my knees go rubbery and I leaned heavily on the desk. "What kind of accident?"

"Car accident."

"Is he. . .?"

"He's alive—so far."

"How did this' happen? How could this happen?" I heard my own voice shrieking in a female pitch and didn't recognize it.

"It was raining, dark. And. . . Dave, it was no accident."

That came as no surprise.

Almost in one breath, he reported the details to me

as they'd been reported to him by Mickey Snelling from Florida. Then he said, "There isn't a doctor on the staff of that hospital that believes it was an accident. They say he must have been bludgeoned, put back in the car, and pushed over the embankment. Dave, are you there?"

"I'm here," I said feebly. Actually, that wasn't strictly true. The restaurant had suddenly taken on a phantasma-gorical aura as if I were floating through a dream. There were haloes around the bottles and glasses behind the bar and the buzzes and clinks and murmurs drifting in from the dining room mingled into a surrealistic cacophony, like electronic music. My ears and toes and fingertips tingled as after the first rush of smoked pot. It seemed as if some psychological safety valve had blown out in my brain to protect me against the unbearable reality of this moment. I listened to the commissioner's gruesome catalogue of Willie's injuries as if through cotton wool.

A waiter walked by with a trayful of drinks. I grabbed the nearest one and tossed it down my throat, hoping it was bourbon. It was Scotch but I didn't care. I told the astonished waiter to put it on my bill and a moment later the hot alcohol seared through the fuzz in my brain like the sun burning off a morning fog.

". . . story we're officially giving out is that it was an accident," the commissioner was saying.

"Of course."

"And we've got to stick to it and make everybody else stick to it—police, doctors, and above all, Willie himself, until we find those fucking bastards. So you've got to grab the next plane to Florida. Jacksonville's your best bet, and I'll arrange for a chopper to take you from there to Nantes."

"And when I get there?"

"See if you can hold everything together. Mickey Snelling will keep the reporters at bay till then."

"Do you really think the press will buy the 'accident' story?"

"Of course not. But until we can get a line on who did this—well, Dave, we may have to kick a lot of ass to keep the lid on it and delay an investigation. You may even have to do some shmearing. The pursestrings for that are wide open."

"I understand. But who do you think. . .?"

"Do me a favor, Dave. Get the hell down there, then call me and ask me all those questions from there. By that time, I'll feel better up to answering them. Right now I'm in a state of shock."

"Sure," I said, wondering what, if he was in a state of shock, was the term for the state I was in. . .

The press, needless to say, did not buy it. But neither did the press get to the bottom of Willie Hesketh's "accident." The medical and investigative personnel connected with the case stuck to their story and withstood the withering barrage of journalistic skepticism that filled the papers and newscasts for days with speculation. It behooves me to say nothing of how this was accomplished but let's just say when the new wings of Nantes General Hospital and the Nantes State Police Headquarters are opened, they ought to be named after Commissioner Bailey.

Of paramount importance is that Willie himself agreed to stick to the "accident" story, too. As soon as he was conscious and coherent, the following morning, I was admitted to his room. The details of that interview are un-bearably painful for me. To have to face this broken ruin of a once-magnificent athlete and press him, through his agony, to deny that he'd been beaten; to promise him in reward for his silence a lifelong pension and the promise of a cushy job in baseball—this was one of the most disgusting pieces of business I've ever undertaken. I came close to puking when

I walked out. But it had to be done because the stakes were nothing less than the good name of baseball.

That night, over a bottle of bourbon, I contemplated the cesspool of greed and stubbornness and stupidity into which the owners and players had sucked Willie to his destruction and I cynically questioned what good name baseball any longer had. Maybe the healthiest thing that could happen would be for the truth to come out, to let the players and owners and public see, in the appalling X-rays of Willie's shattered skeleton, the depths to which the Great American Pastime had fallen. But it was not in me to do this and I hated myself for lacking the balls.

Anyone who follows the sports pages remembers what happened that next week. The reaction on both sides of the conflict was almost universal revulsion and many players were so horrified by what their strike had wrought that they sued for peace or simply entered training camp. Two days later, Sam Metcalf, the firebrand lawyer who headed the Players Association, called an emergency meeting of the player representatives from each team in Houston, Texas, for he realized the strike would rapidly dissolve unless he stiffened the players' spines. But his efforts availed him nothing; the players were running scared and wanted to accept the owners' terms, however disadvantageous.

In a stormy session at the Houston Oaks Hotel, Metcalf made a last-ditch attempt to hold the reps in line. The most dramatic moment came when he read a long telegram he'd received from the president of the Players Association, At-lanta Braves catcher Buddy Gilpin. Gilpin was an outspoken radical whose mishmash of Marxist dialectic, Cajun homilies, and pseudo-hip diddlybop passed for eloquence, though personally speaking, it was pure jive to me. Nevertheless, he had done more than any other figure to keep the players on the picket line. Gilpin had mysteriously absented himself from the emergency meeting but his telegram cleared up the enigma; he had decided to boycott the meeting on the grounds that it had been convened in a mood of hysteria. He pleaded with the players not to yield to fear, to stay on the picket line. The owners, he pleaded, were using the Hesketh incident to crush the strike and the players were playing right into their hands. "Don't Be Duped!" his wire exhorted them. "Don't Be Railroaded! Don't Be Sold Out!"

The telegram was hissed and so was Sam Metcalf reading it. The militance of Gilpin and Metcalf, so popular with the players only a few days ago, was now completely in bad odor.

Metcalf announced that as he obviously no longer commanded the respect and allegiance of the players, he was resigning his position as executive director of the Players Association. The indifference with which this announcement was greeted by the player reps so shattered him that he burst into sobs. Sic transit gloria mundi. An hour later, the reps had elevated a pudgy little trimmer named Sidney Lipsky to the post, and an hour after that, they voted to accept the owners' last offer and go back to spring training.

Chapter III

· · · ·

Which brings me back to that exhibition game in St. Petersburg.

The crowd finally settled down after Willie's departure but the players apparently did not. What had remained a tight 2-1 duel with Jerry Koosman and Bob Apodaca combining to hold the San Francisco Giants to three hits, now broke apart in the eighth inning. The Giants walloped Apodaca for four runs in the top of the eighth and a rookie named Biggs replaced him and put out the fire. Then the Mets came back for two runs in the bottom of the eighth and another in the bottom of the ninth, tying up the game and sending it into extra innings. A lot of fans, cognizant of the Mets' reputation for record-breaking extra-inning games, began to filter out at that point, but I wouldn't have left if the game had gone to thirty innings. Depressed as I was after Willie's appearance, there is no tonic like baseball: exhibition or regular season, major league, minor league, little league, or sandlot. Love that game!

The tenth inning went scoreless for both sides and just as the Mets trotted out to the field for the top of the eleventh, I heard a voice behind me, one as familiar to me as my own, a querulous baritone with a Texas drawl as thick as Aunt Gertie's gravy.

"I suppose you know what a Polack room-divider is," said the voice.

I chuckled in advance of the punch line and slapped my knee. Without bothering to turn around, I said, "No, what's a Polack room-divider?"

"A boiler," came the hissing chortle accompanied, for emphasis, by a bone-rattling slap on my shoulder.

I finally twisted my head around and gazed upon my oldest and closest friend, New York Post sports columnist Roy Lescade. Roy and I had pounded the varnish off each other's helmets for three undergraduate years when he was linebacker for the Texas A&M Aggies and I tight end for the Texas University Longhorns. After graduating, he'd been drafted by the Chicago Bears while I opted to join the army. When I finished my hitch, I fully expected to find him holding down a regular berth with the Bears. But Roy had a lazy streak in him and failed to make the cut, which he says is the best thing that could have happened to him. He capitalized on a natural gift of self-expression and got into sportswriting, eventually landing a regular column with the New York Post.

Roy was not only a helluva writer, he was an honest one. He liked to boast he invented only ten percent of what he wrote, which for a sportswriter is like batting 600. He was a fiercely loyal friend, and above all, a deeply sensitive man. His human-interest stories had copped dozens of journalism prizes and awards. In fact, I owe my life to Roy's depth of humanity, for it was he who tracked me down when I went on my two-year drunken toot and rescued me from the same alcoholic oblivion that had sent half my kinfolk to early graves.

He now loomed over me, a shag rug of a man with a mane of unkempt brown hair and a day's growth of grizzled beard. He wore the same crumpled, stained, khaki raincoat he'd worn for as long as I could remember, a garment for all seasons save the rainy one, for it had long ago lost its water repellency and filled up like a sponge in inclement weather.

I clasped his hand and felt gladder of spirit than I'd felt in weeks. "Roy, would you mind telling me what you have against Polacks?"

"Aw, hell, Lightning," he grinned, addressing me by one of my nicknames, "I have no more against Polacks than I do against Wops, Micks, Hebes, or niggers, leastways not when it comes to a good joke. Like the one about why Italian dogs have pushed-in noses."

"Roy, I don't want to hear the one about why Italian dogs have pushed-in noses."

"Suit yourself."

I sighed and shook my head. "All right, you sonofabitch. Why do Italian dogs have pushed-in noses?"

"From chasing parked cars."

He burst into that wheezing, hissing, hiccoughing laugh, but it was counterpointed by a feminine titter. I hadn't realized up to then that he had a girl with him. I craned my neck and found myself looking into as pretty a pair of blue eyes as you'd ever want to see, twin aquamarines gleaming in the Florida sun. A three-second up-and-down survey disclosed that the setting was as captivating as those semiprecious stones she had for irises. She was a petite kid, maybe five-three, and I don't think she'd have topped the scale at a hundred pounds. But it was all lean meat, the firmness of a girl spang out of teen age, perfectly distributed and packaged in short-shorts and a cotton halter through which poked her nipples like a couple of grapes. Her body was tanned and had the faintest patina of yellow hair. Her face was round and doll-like, with a mouth my grandma liked to call "kissy." Her hair was short and blond and kind of frizzy. Her laughter was all tinkle-bells, high eighth-notes that made you feel happy for no reason at all. She had a tiny gap between two front teeth, reminding me of a pet hamster you wanted to pick up and tickle. I rose out of my seat.

"Say hello to Bonnie Butler," Roy rasped. "Bonnie, this here's Dave Bolt?" Roy had no respect for declarative sentences. He ended half of them with question marks.

"It's a pleasure to make your acquaintance," she said. The phrasing of her salutation and the twang of its delivery fixed her for me immediately.

"Hey, a Texas gal!"

"Down in front!" someone yelled.

I ushered Roy and Bonnie into the empty seats next to me. We watched the game for a moment or two, but my attention had been preempted by this happy little gamine Roy had brought with him. I wondered what was the relationship between them and how I could interfere with it. Roy had stolen so many girls from me, I didn't think he'd mind if I repaid the favor just this once.

"Bonnie's a Brownsville gal?" Roy explained with that upward inflection, referring proudly to his hometown.

"You mean, that tumbledown tank-town on the Meskin border?" I inquired with a wink at my buddy.

Bonnie curled her lip. "I'll have you know that some of the most colorful events in Texas history occurred in Brownsville, Mr. Bolt."

"That's true enough, Dave," Roy took up with a straight face. "The time the Cochran bull left his whang on the barbed wire represents a high point in the winning of the frontier."

Bonnie affected a sulk while he chortled but Roy elbowed her and she issued a grin that was pure Texas sunlight.

"Where'd you find this heifer?" I asked my friend.

"I didn't find her, she found me. She's the niece of a guy I used to hang out with. She's got this problem and came to me with it. Thought a journalist might help her?"

"What kind of problem, if I may ask?"

"You may not only ask, you may help. That's why we come looking for you?"

"That's one reason why you come looking for me," I said. With his typical deviousness, he'd get around to the other before long.

He looked at me as if butter wouldn't melt in his mouth. "I can't imagine what you might be referring to."

I ignored him and looked back at the girl sitting between us. "If Bonnie here's got a problem, I certainly want to render assistance."

"Even if it involves her boyfriend?"

I tried not to let Roy's pinprick puncture my balloon but my face must have revealed my disappointment. He chuckled uncontrollably.

"That's some funny joke, Roy. Who's her boyfriend?"

"Ever hear of Lonnie Raintree?"

I looked into the cerulean Florida sky. I'd heard the name recently but couldn't quite place it.

"You read about him in the Sporting News," Roy prompted. "He's the infielder doing time down at Bristow?" I snapped my fingers with recognition, and the Sporting News article, with its picture of the lean, long-haired, glamorous kid with a face almost as pretty as Bonnie's flashed before my memory like a newsreel. The details were a little vague but I remembered that he'd been one of the hottest infield prospects the Texas League had produced in a long time, with a batting average in the high three hundreds, thirty or forty home runs, and an arm like a rocket launcher. Scouting reports on him had read like reviews of My Fair Lady and a number of major league teams had been romancing him when a Texas Ranger, acting on an anonymous tip, picked him up for drug possession. I think they'd found several bags of unprocessed grass in the hubcaps of his car, something like that.

I looked at Bonnie with furrowed eyebrows. "I'd have thought you'd have more sense to get involved with something like that, young lady."

"And I'd have thought you had better manners than to judge someone before you know the facts, Mr. Bolt." Bonnie's eyes blazed with Irish fire and I stammered an apology. "The fact is, Lonnie was framed. He doesn't know pot from pecans. I should know. I've gone with him for three years."

"Well, then, how'd the dope get in his hubcaps? It didn't grow there of its own accord."

"Someone put it in there and then called Ranger Geary."

"Someone with a grudge against him, you mean?"

"Yes."

"Do you know who?"

"No."

"But you're convinced it's a frameup?"

"Sure as God made little green apples."

"Does Lonnie have an idea who?"

"If he did, don't you think he'd say?"

"Probably would, probably would," I admitted. I gestured with my chin at Roy. "Where does Smokey the Bear here come in?"

"I thought Roy could publicize this injustice, being as how he's an influential journalist."

"And I agreed," Roy said.

"For your usual price?"

"Mr. Lescade never said anything about doing this for money," Bonnie said indignantly.

"I wasn't referring to money," I said.

Bonnie looked up at me, moisture clouding those aquamarine eyes and chin quivering just this side of a cry and I realized my teasing had gone too far. "Roy told me you were a compassionate man. I guess this is what he meant."

I apologized again, more elaborately. This was really no joking matter, at least not for Bonnie. Her man was in jail and she was at the end of her tether. I felt bad, so bad I let my guilt overrule my good senses, "I don't know how I can help but I'll do whatever I can," I promised.

Amazing how quick her tears dried up. Two big sniffs and she was chirping thirteen to the dozen. "Well, see, Roy has talked to Warden DePaw and Governor Bondy and Judge Hickman, that's the one who tried Lonnie. And they are willing to bend over backwards to reconsider the case if we can come up with some hard evidence to support what Lonnie's claiming about being framed. I was hoping Roy here could dig up that evidence and write, y'know, like a column in his paper or something? Or maybe get it into Time magazine? But he says he doesn't have time because he has to return to New York to cover the Knicks and Rangers and stuff. But he did say you might help out on account of you've got a warm spot in your heart for Texas folks and maybe Lonnie would let you become his agent if you got him out."

I threw Roy a dirty look. "Roy, you know perfectly well I'm up to my hips in the Willie Hesketh case."

"I certainly do and that's the other thing I wanted to talk to you about."

"As if I couldn't have guessed."

"I'll be glad to pay your expenses," Bonnie offered.

"To visit your boyfriend? Oh, that's all right," I said. "I've got to go to Texas anyway, on some other business."

"Then you'll do it?" She jumped up and down, clapping her hands like a teenybopper at an Alice Cooper concert.

"I guess. There's something poetic about a couple of lovers named Lonnie and Bonnie. It would make a terrific ballad."

She hugged me and planted a big wet kiss on my cheek. I felt like Santa Claus at Macy's. "How can I thank you, Mr. Bolt?"

"You really want to thank me? Tell your shabby friend over there that I'm not answering his questions about Willie Hesketh."

"Now wait a minute, Dave," Roy whined.

"Sorry, buddy. You've won your share of favors off me for one day."

Roy shook his head. "I knew I should of left you for dead when I had the chance."

"Besides, there's nothing to tell. Willie Hesketh wrecked his car in an auto accident on a slippery road."

"Sure. And the Watergate plumbers was only looking for a men's room when they wandered into Democratic headquarters. The truth—"

"The truth is for me to know and you to find out," I snapped.

As soon as I'd issued this challenge, I wanted to take it back. Roy stiffened, his eyes narrowed to squints, and his jaw seemed to square off with single-minded resolution. I'd seen that look on Roy's face before and knew that when he set his mind to it, nothing could stop him from getting his story. Half the reporters in the country had been digging into the case and had come up empty-handed but I knew my wily old friend would find the bottom of it. What the hell, with nothing to go on but a faint odor of alcohol, he'd managed to track me down over seven southwestern states.

I reached across Bonnie's lap and patted Roy's knee. "I'll tell you what, old buddy. You keep your bloodhounds in the kennel for a couple of weeks and I'll give you something exclusive."

"Then you admit—"

"I don't admit shit, pardon my French," I said with a remorseful glance at Bonnie. "But just supposing it was not an accident, there are a million good reasons why it would be harmful for the truth to come out before its time. If you're willing to cool it a while and go home and do your little boilerplate stories on Walt Frazier's ailing big toe and Eddie Giacomin's ailing little finger, I'll see to it that the gods shed their bounty on you with open hands—at the right time. Fair enough?"

"Fair enough."

"Good. Then let's watch the ballgame."

"The ballgame?" Bonnie laughed. "Boys, the ballgame's been over for ten minutes."

Chapter IV

• • • •

That night I enriched the American Telephone & Telegraph Company to the tune of sixty-one dollars and ninety cents in a phone conversation with Commissioner Bailey that lasted the length of the Knicks-Bucks game, which I watched out of the corner of my eye on the television set in my Holiday Inn motel room. Bailey and I had discussed the Hesketh situation several times, reviewing suspects and motives and shaping a strategy for investigation. Tonight, we narrowed the scope of the inquiry to manageable proportions and fixed on a solid plan. Tomorrow, I was to get to work.

I say 'solid plan" as if it were Operation Overlord, but the truth is, it was scarcely solider than a bowl of jellied madrilène.

Broadly, there were three categories of people with a vested interest in seeing Willie Hesketh mauled. First, it might have been some players from the radical fringe of strikers, Buddy Gilpin or some of the malcontents that clung to his coattails. Their motive was certainly the most comprehensible one: Willie threatened the unity of their strike. And Willie's assailants did, it will be remembered, use baseball bats. And that was the trouble: the obviousness of it was... well... too obvious, as if someone wanted people to think it had been ballplayers. Still, this possibility had to be run down.

Second, it could have been the Federation of Skilled Workers, the union with which the Players Association had just signed a secret "mutual interest" pact. Anxious to display their power, the union might have taken it upon itself to send some goons down to Florida to intercept Willie and make an example of him for any other potential scab to see. If Pinky Ryan, the head of the FSW, had figured that the same tactics that prevailed in the coal and steel and teamster and stevedore unions could prevail for baseball players, he had made a misjudgment that would be hysterically funny if it hadn't resulted in the vegetablization of a beautiful human being. In fact, it was a misjudgment so gross it was almost impossible for me to believe that anything less than a crowning imbecile could have made it. And from what I'd heard about Pinky Ryan, he was anything but a crowning imbecile. So this possibility, too, seemed almost too obvious to be true.

Finally, we wondered if it might have been one of the owners: at least, that was not too obvious! Indeed, it was almost too far-out to merit serious consideration. But here is how we reasoned: this hypothetical owner must have perceived that the beating of Willie would so horrify and divide the striking ballplayers that they would no longer want to continue their action and the strike would collapse. Which is precisely what did happen. Perhaps, then, there was among the owners a man who felt that this end justified any means.

But it was hard for us to believe that such a thing could happen in this day and age. It might have in the freewheeling days earlier in the century when owners were feudal barons who stopped at nothing to hold their serfs in bondage. But today? I just couldn't see it. Say what you will about owners, I don't think most of them are capable of conceiving such Machiavellian plots and even fewer are capable of executing them. Once again, however, we were obliged at least to check out the possibility.

In any case, we had one solid piece of evidence to go by, and one only: somewhere out there, a man was walking around with one eye. "I've got every available man combing the hospitals, clinics, and doctors in the north Florida area." the commissioner said. "The guy must have shown up somewhere around there."

"I'm sure he did," I said, "but the odds are against us discovering who treated him. If he and his pals were professional gangsters, they undoubtedly found some hack croaker on mob payroll to treat him and there'd be no records kept. Also likely is that our one-eyed friend would be sent to some secluded spot for recuperation. He might be out of circulation for years. Keep plugging, Commissioner, but don't hold your breath."

"You'll call me from Pittsburgh?"

"You bet."

Pittsburgh was the headquarters of the Federation of Skilled Workers. The commissioner had mailed me a file of clippings on the union and as my Allegheny Airlines 727 dipped its wings for the approach to Greater Pittsburgh International Airport, I shut the file and gazed down at this city of bizarre contrasts. The gleaming towers of the Golden Triangle at the junction of the Allegheny and Monongahela, Gateway Center and Equitable Plaza and the Pittsburgh Hilton presiding over the chartreuse of Point State Park in its early spring foliage, stood like aristocratic ladies preserving their petticoats from the filthy jumble of steel mills, coal pits, rail yards, ash pits, and decayed housing wreathed in gray smoke, that pressed this gorgeous revitalized inner city from beyond its many bridges.

I glimpsed Three Rivers Stadium gliding beneath the starboard wing, then closed my eyes to meditate on my immediate task.

The Federation of Skilled Workers was a union of recent vintage, a rump of the United Steelworkers that had severed its connection in 1968 over differences about the automation of the steel industry. The parent union had been slow to welcome the automation of certain technological processes on the grounds that it would wipe out a lot of jobs. But two of the United Steelworkers' lieutenants, Pinky Ryan and Mark Fioretta, saw an opportunity to organize the small but important battalion of electronics specialists who were seeking a wedge into the industry. So the two broke with their union and formed one of their own.

They managed to secure management support and in due time established a beachhead. With amazing speed, they picked up other unorganized shops and became a force to contend with. However, Ryan and Fioretta quarreled over tactics, Fioretta being the more militant and aggressive and not, it was said, above hooliganism. Pinky wanted no part of Fioretta's monkey business, so they parted company, Pinky staying with the FSW, Fioretta taking some locals with him to start his own union, the United Craftsmen's Brotherhood. There was no love lost between the two. Early in the 1970s, both unions began courting player organizations in football and baseball and when the baseball strike took shape, both stepped up their efforts to secure affiliation. Ryan's efforts had proved the more successful and culminated in the secret agreement with the Players Association.

That was as much as I knew, except that the secretary-treasurer of the FSW was named Fiona Ryan, undoubtedly a relative placed on the payroll for doing nothing but spending union dues on monthly shopping sprees in Palm Beach.

I had phoned Ryan from St. Petersburg and he'd offered to pick me up at the airport and as I muscled through the crowd at gate 14, I searched for a man who fitted my imagination's image of an Irish union organizer in a steel town. He would be short and stocky with reddish-brown hair, a pink-flourished face (why else would he be called Pinky?), with freckles, and would chomp on the stub of a cheap fat stogie while talking with a Barry Fitzgerald accent. And what the hell, as long as I was conjuring up stereotypes, he might as well wear a derby hat.

Small surprise that no one even vaguely fitting this description stepped out of the crowd to greet me. What did step out was a tall razorblade of a man with shiny black hair who looked a little like John Carradine. His eyes were shrewd and cold and unimpressed. He was impeccably dressed in a three-piece serge suit of heavy cloth and bore an expensive camelhair coat and silk scarf over his left arm. He clasped my hand as he uttered my name and his grip was scarcely what one would have expected of a steel-drivin' man. His hand felt funny and when I withdrew mine I noticed that his pinky was severed at the first knuckle, probably in a mill accident. And that, not the color of his face, was where his nickname came from. The almost stagy diction of his greeting bespoke someone from Oxford or Cambridge rather than Dublin.

So much for my image of Pinky Ryan.

He twiddled his fingers at someone standing on the perimeter of the crowd. His signal was acknowledged by a white hand which, as we broke clear of the throng, turned out to belong to a lithe, lovely redhead with a face out of a Constable portrait. She was dressed in a soft green tweed suit over a darker, forest green sweater. Oddly enough, the conservatism of her clothing only stimulated my interest, instead of quelling it.

Her face was a milk-white oval with a faint bridge of freckles across her nose and cheekbones. Her eyes were sea-green but I could have asked their expression to be a little less severe. And as long as I was wishing, I could have wished for a warm smile. But she eyed me with sharp suspicion that was not even slightly disarmed by the big-as-all-outdoors cowboy smile I flashed at her. In fact, a red tint swept up her graceful white throat and rouged her cheeks but there was no mistaking this blush for modesty, it was hostility all the way.

"I'd like you to meet my daughter Fiona, Mr. Bolt. She's the executive secretary of the FSW."

Something told me the offer of a handshake would be re-buffed, so I simply nodded and proffered a how-do-you-do.

She nodded back with frosty formality. I studied her face another moment and recognized resemblances to her father. It's not that their features were alike—these must have derived from her mother, and what a beauty she must have been!—but their attitudes. Both were stolid and dour. I don't know if that was their natural expression or whether it was specially laid on for my benefit but either way, I felt uncomfortable. I made up my mind to conduct my interview with them with the caution of a snake-handler extracting toxin from a rattler.

It was easy enough to understand their antagonism. I'd bluntly stated my purpose when I called from St. Petersburg: I was coming seeking a possible link between the FSW and the people who'd beaten up my client. Still, I'd have liked to divorce my business from the pleasure of looking into Fiona Ryan's eyes because a smile on that cameo face would have reduced me to the consistency of tapioca pudding.

"Do you have any other luggage?" Ryan asked, gesturing with his pointed chin at the small valise I'd carried off the plane.

"No, this is it. I wasn't planning to stay long."

"That's good," Ryan said. The glimmer of a wink or smile could have turned it into a joke. But he gave me nothing more than the raw rudeness of the remark.

We walked to the parking lot, Ryan and daughter ahead of me, leaving me to trail like an unwanted stepchild. We arrived at their car, a late-model Olds sedan and after putting my bag in the trunk Ryan ushered me into the back seat. Then he got into the driver's seat and Fiona into the passenger's and we drove in utter silence along the Penn-Lincoln Expressway all the way into the city. They never once turned around, asked me a question, commented on the weather, or acknowledged my existence. It was a deliberate strategy to make me feel unwelcome and uneasy and it was totally effective. I watched the drab scenery flit by and pretended indifference but I could feel my anxiety level rising.

We crossed the Monongahela over the Fort Pitt Bridge and up Liberty Avenue, which flanked the stupendous twenty-three-acre Gateway Center complex. The headquarters of the FSW were located on the fifteenth floor of the Westinghouse Building, looking out over the point. The offices were not particularly large but were well furnished and attractive, though not flashy. I imagine union leaders have to tread a difficult path when they decorate their headquarters; the place must look substantial enough to suggest success and power and influence, but not so ostentatious as to make a rank-and-file member ask what the hell his dues are being applied to. The solid but unornate décor of the FSW seemed to strike that balance. Instead of paintings, Ryan had hung photographs on the walls, blowups of Pittsburgh landmarks like the University of Pittsburgh's Cathedral of Learning, Mellon Square Park, the Carnegie Museum, and Phipps Conservatory. There was also a picture of Forbes Field, the old home of the Pirates. If Ryan wanted to impress baseball folks, he should have known better than to keep that anachronism up there.

Ryan's office itself was large, bright, and simple, with a splendid view of Point State Park and the junction of the rivers beyond. It had a bar and there was a humidor on his desk, but Ryan, seating himself behind his ponderous and rather unkempt desk, offered me neither drink nor tobacco. He simply tugged at his cuffs and looked at me expectantly. Fiona took a chair beside him, crossed her legs and skewered me with an unfriendly stare. To cap off this discourteous treatment, Ryan looked at his watch.

They were going to place the burden of this interview squarely on my shoulders. I was about to hit them with my first question when I got an idea.

If they were going to stare at me, I'd stare right back at them. And that's just what I did, saying nothing.

For a minute we were deadlocked, our eyes clinched in a staring contest, like a game of optical chicken to see who would swerve first. Then my gambit began to tell. First Ryan, then Fiona, dropped their eyes, looked up again, looked at each other, looked back at me, and shifted in their seats. Ryan's fingers started to twiddle and Fiona began brushing a hand through her luxuriant red hair. The more nervous they got, the cooler I got. Ryan looked at his watch again and began a tattoo on his desktop with his well-manicured fingernails.

The game of chicken worked. I got him to swerve first. "You have some business with us, Mr. Bolt?"

"I've already stated my business, Mr. Ryan."

"I have nothing to contribute to your inquiry," he said.

I rose. "Then I guess I'll be moving on," I said. They blinked uncomprehendingly. I crossed to the door and put my hand on the knob. "Oh, yes, can I trouble you for a favor? Would you mind having your secretary call the Attorney General's office in Washington and tell him my meeting in Pittsburgh has ended earlier than I'd expected and I can see him this afternoon instead of tomorrow morning?"

Ryan swallowed loudly. "The Attorney General?"

I shrugged. "Yes. We'd been hoping to keep our inquiry small and informal but now it looks like Uncle Sam will have to step in."

Ryan got the message. After exchanging glances with Fiona, he said, "Well, now, as long as you've come to Pittsburgh specially to see us. . ."

"Oh, that's all right," I said, laying it on a trifle thick. "I know you have pressing appointments."

"Please sit down, Mr. Bolt," he commanded, trying not to make it sound like a plea.

I shrugged and took my seat again.

He got up and went to the bar. "What's your pleasure?"

"Bourbon—and civility."

"We only have bourbon," he replied with a thin smile.

"Look again."

He made himself a Scotch and soda and Fiona a whiskey neat. At which I raised an eyebrow.

"Fiona's a throwback to her grandfather. She drinks like a shantytown Mick."

"How does she swear?"

"I suspect you'll have an opportunity to find out for yourself," he replied, smiling a wee bit more broadly. He looked at Fiona, who tossed the shot of whiskey down her throat without a flinch and eyed me impatiently.

"Now, Mr. Bolt," Ryan said refilling Fiona's glass and settling down into his chair, "you told me you wanted to discuss your client's accident with me. What earthly reason. . .?"

I held up my hands. "I think it would save a great deal of time if we didn't play coy with one another, Mr. Ryan. So let's cut through the blarney. During the baseball strike your union began earnest negotiations with the Major Leagues Players Association with a view to creating some sort of affiliation. On March 14th, the Players Association signed a letter of mutual interest with you, pledging cooperation between the two unions. Shortly thereafter, my client, Willie Hesketh, announced his determination to cross the players' picket line and enter training camp. Two days subsequent to that announcement, he was found beaten within an inch of his life, his arms, legs, and the fingers of his right hand deliberately smashed to render him incapable of ever playing baseball again. Now, I've come to find out what connection, if any, there is between that crime and your union's activities."

I'd studied Ryan's eyes when I mentioned the beating. I'm not sure what response I sought or expected but what I got was the eye of a fish. "The newspapers have given out the story that Hesketh was hurt in an accident," he said levelly.

"Yes, that certainly is the story they've given out. Now, what's the story you're giving out?"

In reply, he spun in his chair and slid a walnut wall panel back to reveal the door of a small safe. He spun the combination dial several times, then wrenched open the door. He waved a finger over several sheaves of papers, then tapped one and pulled it out. He removed a rubber band and handed me the topmost sheet.

It was a letter on office stationery and when I unfolded it I noted the logo of the Players Association. My eyes swept down the page, where I found the signatures of Sam Metcalf, executive director of the Players Association, and Buddy Gilpin, president of the Players Association. Below these were the signatures of Pinky Ryan and Fiona Ryan, and still further down the page, the signatures and seal of a notary. In fact, most of the letter was taken up by signatures. The text itself was but two or three paragraphs, mostly Whereases. I scanned down to the last paragraph, the kicker. Following the phrase "Therefore, it is mutually agreed and covenanted. . ." was a statement of "common interests" and a pledge of "concerted action" that for eloquent vagueness was second only to the Preamble to the United States Constitution.

I tossed the letter back at Ryan. "Do you really think I expected you to state in writing that you would mutilate any baseball player who crossed the picket line?"

"Mr. Bolt!" It had been so long since Fiona had spoken that her voice startled me. Her face as red as a beefsteak tomato and the ligaments of her throat tight with anger.

"Now, now, Fiona," Ryan placated her.

"Don't now-now me, Daddy. Do you know what this jerk is accusing us of?"

"He hasn't accused us of anything yet," Daddy said.

"What does he have to do, dump shit on your head to make you understand what he's trying to pin on us?"

Ryan looked at me helplessly and I almost felt a camaraderie for the poor beleaguered guy. He may have been a big shot in all other respects, but Fiona owned his heartstrings.

She wasn't through by any means. She turned her blazing eyes on me again and snorted, "If you hadn't put your client up to breaking the strike—"

"That will be enough, Fiona," Ryan finally said with some firmness.

"I'd like to slap his face!" she snarled, downing her second glass of whiskey and fumbling in her handbag for a cigarette. She lit it with trembling fingers.

Ryan smiled at me. "I told you, Mr. Bolt—a throwback to her shantytown ancestry. They say personality skips every other generation."

Fiona had really hurt me with that crack about putting Willie up to crossing the picket line and I was smoldering. But I counted to ten and decided I'd have a go at conciliating her before lunging at her throat and throttling her.

"I'm sorry, Miss Ryan but as you can imagine, the Willie Hesketh incident means a great deal to me."

"Yes, the loss of a commission."

I winced. "I see you learned street-fighting from your grandfather, too." I turned away from her and looked back at her father. "I'm sure you must know how far beyond the question of commissions this matter goes."

"No one understands better than I, Mr. Bolt. It resulted in the cancellation of the agreement you just read. The day after your client's 'accident,' the Players Association severed its association with us. I lost perhaps the most important gain I'd ever achieved. I have that letter in the safe, too, if you'd like to read it, the letter of cancellation."

He started to turn to the safe but I shook my head. When he looked back at me again his face had transformed. His mouth was pulled down at the corners and his eyes were hazy with moisture. This thing had obviously hit him pretty hard. I darted a glance in Fiona's direction. Her eyes were filled with tears and she was groping in her bag for a tissue. She'd surrendered to the emotion her father was struggling to contain. I felt a lump forming in my gullet and dropped my eyes to seek lint on the knees of my trousers.

Fiona sniffed, found a tissue, and dabbed her eyes and

nose with it. Then she brushed back her hair and shook her head as if shedding the human weakness that had momentarily overcome her. When she spoke, her voice was firm once again. "Mr. Bolt, even supposing that our Federation was not above using violence to get its way, do you really think we could be so stupid as to do the very thing that would destroy our chance of forming a firm, lasting bond with the Players Association?"

The question thrust to the heart of it. "Well," I confessed, "you two seem anything but stupid."

Fiona laughed. "Thank you for the gracious compliment." It was a bitter laugh but it was the first time I'd heard a laugh of any kind from her and I felt oddly relieved. I think I'd have been heartbroken if she were devoid of a sense of humor, however cynical.

"If you'd allow me, I'd pay you many more," I said.

I could see a sarcastic reply forming on her lips but she checked herself. What stopped her, I don't know. Maybe she recognized that the role of Grand Inquisitor sat very poorly with me. Whatever it was, her eyes softened, and she slumped a little, as if very weary.

"I've got to tell you," I followed up, "that it seemed unlikely to us—the commissioner and me, I mean—that you'd do anything as reckless as that. But I had to hear it from you, you understand."

"Yes," she said. And after an interval: "Mr. Bolt, do you really want to get to the bottom of this?"

"Yes, of course."

"Well, so do we."

"But you've got to trust us," her father chimed in. "You've got to believe that we had as much at stake as you did. You've got to believe that we want to bring the men who did this to justice as much as you do."

I quietly mulled it over. Both my brain and the seat of my pants, the latter being where I make most of my important decisions, told me I'd been fishing in the wrong waterhole. That these two would cut off their noses to spite their faces just didn't make sense. There might be much to be gained by trusting them. But, as my daddy was fond of saying, Trust everybody but cut the cards. I would accept their protests of innocence for now but reserve ten percent skepticism against the possibility of hidden motives that might surface later.

"Do you have any ideas who might possibly have attacked Willie?" I asked.

An interesting thing happened. Just as Fiona opened her mouth to reply, her father stiffened slightly and a glance passed between them. She seemed to censor what she had been about say. "A few," she substituted with studied casualness.

Her father had signaled her off but I decided not to call them on it for the moment. I merely asked, "Like what?"

"'We'd like to check them out on our own before troubling you," Ryan said.

"There's no point in both of us going over the same ground," I answered.

"I don't think there's much chance of that," Ryan said.

Fiona spoke. "What about you, Mr. Bolt? What other leads do you have? Besides us," she added wryly.

"The only solid lead we have is that one of the gorillas who beat up Willie lost an eye in the struggle. We're checking doctors who might have treated him."

"I see," Fiona said with a sour face at the thought of somebody poking somebody else's eye out.

"Our main thrust," I continued, "is the ballplayers themselves. The beating was administered with baseball bats."

"Anyone can use a baseball bat," Ryan averred. "In fact, that's just the weapon someone might use to make you pin the rap on ballplayers."

"I'm aware of that but even if they'd used shillelaghs, we'd be obliged to suspect ballplayers, for obvious reasons."

"It should be easy enough to find a major league ballplayer who lost an eye recently," Fiona pointed out.

"Not quite so. At the moment there are twenty or twenty-five ballplayers who have not shown up for spring training. Most of them are contract holdouts, but a few are sick, wrapping up off-season jobs, moving their households from one town to another, that kind of thing. On the other hand, one of them may be walking around with half his God-given complement of eyeballs."

Fiona's face wrinkled up in disgust again.

"Then you'll be chasing down those holdouts," Ryan said.

"The League has already chased half of them down. The other half are still incommunicado for one reason or another. I have a little list," I said, tapping the breast pocket of my blazer. "We're also looking into the possibility that an owner engineered this."

"I thought of that myself," said Ryan.

"That seems a little incredible to me," Fiona volunteered with a shake of her head. Her red hair swirled off one shoulder and settled on the other.

"No doubt it is," I said. "But like I said before, there was a tremendous amount at stake in this strike. The owners, as you know, were actually contemplating shutting down the season. Some of them would have been bankrupted. One of them might have gotten pretty desperate and engineered this scheme."

Fiona still looked incredulous. "I don't think we can discount it," her father said to her. "Management is management, whether it be steel mills or baseball teams. There are precedents for the kind of treachery Mr. Bolt has alluded to. And we know that a number of club owners have connections that might be termed dubious, to say the least." He looked at his watch, then at me apologetically. "I really do have an appointment. Fiona, maybe you'd like to drive Mr. Bolt back out to the airport."

"I was hoping to grab some lunch," I said.

"Well, then, Fiona," he said getting to his feet, "maybe you'd like to take Mr. Bolt to lunch."

I thought I detected a satirical twinkle in his eyes. Fiona made a face.

"I don't think she's much inclined, Mr. Ryan," I said.

"Of course she is, aren't you, darling?"

"Daddy," she sighed, "sometimes. . ." She looked at me. "Of course I am."

Chapter V

· · · ·

We taxied over to the William Penn, a heavy old hotel across the street from lovely Mellon Square, and dined in a handsome oak-paneled room with high leaded windows and gorgeous chandeliers. It must have been a haven for industrial barons of yore but the new breed preferred to dine in the stainless steel and glass delights of Gateway Center. I was glad Fiona had chosen this anachronism; I treasure old fashion whenever I come across it, both in buildings and people.

Fiona sat across the table from me, aimlessly tapping her shot glass with a long fingernail. She looked uncomfortable, almost miserable.

"I really didn't intend to inveigle you into coming to lunch with me," I said. "After all, just half an hour ago you were ready to slap my face, or worse."

She raked her hair with graceful fingers. "Oh, it wasn't that. It's just that Daddy—well, he sometimes plays games."

"Aha. You mean, like matchmaking."

She laughed uneasily. "Yes. He's always scouting up mates for me."

"Nothing wrong with that."

"Everything's wrong with it. I'm not looking, for one thing. And for another, he wouldn't know what to do if I did find somebody."

"He depends on you, huh?"

"Oh, totally. But he feels guilty about it at the same time. He's afraid he's going to make an old maid out of me."

"I'd say you have a way to go before that happens."

"That's what I keep telling him. I'm only twenty-six, after all. And I've seen what happens to people who marry too young."

"So have I."

She tilted her head attentively. "You sound like you're referring to yourself."

"I am," I said. She seemed to be leaving it up to me to elaborate or not and I decided to leave it alone.

Like the pain in my ankles from the injury that had put me out of football, my remorse about Nancy, my ex-wife, and Jody, our daughter, now aged nine, waxed and waned. There were stretches of time when I didn't think about them at all. There were others when, again, like my ankles, the memory of what we'd had throbbed quietly. And sometimes that memory flared up so sharply I went into depression for days. In fact, I'd noticed over the years a correlation between the two, the physical injury and the less tangible one to my emotions. In the damp cold of winter my legs, in spite of their rehabilitation through therapy and exercise, bothered me so much I limped noticeably. And those were the times when the recollection of the marriage I'd destroyed through my own intemperance gnawed at me so angrily I could hardly function.

In terms of both, this had been the worst winter yet. My arrangement with Nancy called for my getting custody of

Jody over the Christmas holidays but a crisis had come up that required me to fly to the West Coast, so Jody had stayed with her mother. My guilt had practically eaten me alive, and my legs, during the protracted spell of lousy weather in January and February, had murdered me, as if exacting punishment for my neglect of the kid.

"Let's order," I said.

The business of studying the menu provided a welcome distraction from my somber thoughts and after giving our order to the waiter, we picked up new threads. Fiona talked about her father, her green eyes kindling almost unnaturally in the dim light of the restaurant. "This was the worst setback of his life," she said. "You see, Dave—is it all right if I call you Dave?"

"Hell, yes," I beamed.

There went that blush again. Her cheeks were a barometer of her inner life. She seemed to have a blush for every emotion. You could tell from the shade of crimson and the height the blood rose to on her throat and face just what was going on inside her.

"You see," she began again, "what you failed to appreciate when you stormed into our office with your accusations"—she raised a hand to quell the protest on my lips—"is that my father is not cut from the same cloth as the typical labor organizer. For one thing, he's a man of enormous integrity. He's accomplished what he's accomplished honorably and if you know anything at all about labor unionism you'll realize that that's no mean feat. Gangster tactics are not in his repertoire. In fact, that's exactly why he split up with his partner a couple of years ago. They didn't see eye to eye on means."

Her hands had come to life as she talked and they swept through the sky over our table like a pair of swallows.

"For another thing," she went on, "he's a man of vision. His dream was not merely a union of baseball players but of all professional athletes, a union so tightly bonded and blended into the rest of our Federation that no owner, no group of owners, would dare thwart the players in one sport for fear of provoking a work stoppage in sports across the board—to say nothing of stoppages in other industries."

I whistled. "That's what I'd call vision, all right."

"I gather you find that distasteful."

"Terrifying is what I find it."

She arched an eyebrow. "I'm surprised to hear that. I'd have imagined a man in your profession would support that goal wholeheartedly, since it's harmonious with everything you work toward. Or don't you agree that the inequities that all but a privileged few athletes endure—"

I cut her off with a slash of my hand. "Fiona, I agree with everything you're about to say. But I've done a lot of thinking since the strike began and do you know what I've concluded? I've concluded that all this quarreling about inequities and injustices, low starting salaries and reserve clauses and pensions and fringe benefits and freedom issues, high overhead and inflation and television money and box office money and endorsement money and World Series money and money, money, money, money—it's all beside the point."

She gazed at me with one eyebrow arched in a tall inverted V. "And what is the point?"

"The point, darling, is that sports are fun—F. U. N. See, whatever other reasons athletes participate in sports, they also do it for fun. A lot of people tend to forget that and I suppose I'm as guilty of it as anyone else. But you shouldn't underestimate the power of fun—hell, ask any fan. But fun is precisely what's gone out of sports the last few years and that's why I find your father's 'vision' so almighty scary.

Because all it does is take us even further away from fun than we are now. I mean, when a ballplayer takes his life in his hands, as Willie Hesketh did, just because he feels like walking into training camp to play ball—well, then, I say unto you, verily, that ain't no fun, baby."

She leaned on her chin and looked morosely at the tablecloth. "I hadn't thought of it that way."

"I can see that," I said. "Because frankly, Fiona, though I haven't known you an hour, I can tell you're a gal who doesn't have much fun, either."

Her eyes flashed and blinked and I knew I'd scored a bull's-eye. "I suppose I should be insulted, but oddly, I'd been thinking the same thing lately. Only, I'd marked it down to fatigue. I work very, very hard for my father."

"And for yourself?"

She shrugged. "I sometimes find it impossible to distinguish between his interests and my own. I often wonder if my dedication. . ." Suddenly her eyes widened and narrowed and her mouth pulled down in a look of distress. She was looking at something over my left shoulder. I started to turn around but she said, "Don't."

"Someone you don't want to see?"

"Yes."

"From the blush on your throat I'd say it's an old boy-friend."

"God, no! Do me a favor? Move your chair a little to the. . . oh, hell, here he comes."

I twisted in my chair and saw a tall, well-dressed man with wavy silver hair and a Florida suntan pushing away from a table with two smooth-haired men and a blond bimbo whose coiffure seemed to have been fixed with polyurethane plastic—so hard, bullets bounce off it, as the television commercial says.

"Hello, Fiona," the man said. His voice was as well-modulated and unctuous as the public address announcer at a half-time ceremony.

"Hello, Mark," Fiona said grudgingly, trying not to look at him.

"What a pleasant coincidence," he said.

"For whom?"

"Oh, come on. Whatever differences your father and I have had have never applied to you and me."

"Speak for yourself."

The man looked at me as if to appeal Fiona's decision. His smile was plastic and seemed to have nothing to do with the expression of sharp curiosity in his eyes as he studied me. I realized that this was Mark Fioretta, Pinky Ryan's former partner in the labor union, now his competitor.

"I was going to invite you and your friend—to whom I haven't been introduced—to join us for lunch."

"That is the very last thing in the world I would do," Fiona said, glowering at her plate.

Fioretta looked at me again and I said, "The lady has spoken. I think your guests are getting restless."

"Yes. Well, I'm sorry I won't have the pleasure, Mr. . .?"

He extended his hand and I grasped it. "I'm sorry, too."

He wheeled and walked away, throwing me a last dirty look over his shoulder.

I looked at Fiona, who was actually trembling with rage. "I get the impression he's not your favorite person in the whole wide world."

"I hate his bloody guts."

"Just because of your father's feud with him?"

"I'd really rather not talk about it. He's already ruined my lunch."

"If you'd rather go somewhere else. . .?"

"Never. Let him go somewhere else."

I moved my chair over to block her vision of Fioretta and started jollying her along with some Irish jokes I knew, and after a while, I had her distracted and almost completely relaxed. Lunch arrived and her appetite had not been as fatally affected as she claimed. She consumed all of a chef's salad, I a tender veal piccata, and we compromised our differences about wine with a chilled rosé. In due time she forgot about Fioretta and was chattering away. Occasionally her superficial table-talk eyes would deepen into a scrutiny of my face and I could tell she was looking at me for the first time as a man.

We drifted back to the subject we'd been on when Fioretta had interrupted us. "What do you do for fun, Dave?"

"I go to ballgames."

She frowned. "I used to love going, but I never get to them anymore. I just don't have time."

"You might see things in a whole other light if you went to one once in a while."

"I suppose you're right," she said, but insincerely.

"But you won't really do it, will you?"

"Oh, I guess if someone asked me. . ."

"Good. There's a hockey game this afternoon, Pittsburgh Penguins and St. Louis Blues. If we skip dessert we can get to the Civic Arena before it begins." I signaled the waiter for the check.

"It's been taken care of by Mr. Fioretta," he said.

She scathed the poor waiter with her eyes. "You tell Mr. Fioretta. . ." She canceled her first thought, then reached into her purse and pulled out a twenty-dollar bill. "This is for you. Tell Mr. Fioretta that this one is my treat and put both lunches on my account. Take no for an answer and I'll have you fired."

The waiter blanched. "Yes, ma'am."

I blanched a little myself. She was playing a strange game whose rules I didn't understand. Not yet, at any rate.

If anyone had told me I would end up taking Fiona Ryan to bed, I'd have laughed in his face. Not that I hadn't desired her from the first but I'd rated my chances of spending the night with her about equal to the Texas Rangers winning the pennant, and brother, those are dismal odds! My invitation to the hockey game was strictly what I'd said it was, nothing more than an offer to bring a little fun into a life which was obviously atrophying for want of it. Make that two lives—my own hadn't exactly been a rollicking romp for the last six months.

Even after the game, dining at the Carlton House, or after that, catching Lou Rawls at the Holiday House out in Monroeville, or yet after that at a new discotheque in Gateway Center, I couldn't regard seriously the possibility of sex. Oh, she loosened up at every station of our day together, shouting abandonedly at the game, laughing and getting slightly tipsy at dinner, stomping her feet for Lou Rawls at Holiday House, dancing loosely and sensually at the discotheque. Yet throughout it all, she maintained a veneer of reserve in which there wasn't to be found the remotest hint of what was to come. Which was fine with me. It gave me pleasure just to see her enjoying herself and filled an otherwise boring and lonely evening for a bachelor given lately to brooding.

Believe it or not, even when she invited me up to her flat in the handsome Allegheny Towers on Stanwix and Fort Duquesne Boulevard, I received not the vaguest intimation of a crumbling of the ultimate barrier. I took it simply as her desire to prolong an enjoyable evening and that's the spirit in which I accepted the invitation. She made me coffee and Sara Lee pineapple cheesecake and we chatted in the warm, earth-colored living room of her apartment about a lot of trivial things. It was not until I got up to leave that she enclosed my wrist with strong fingers. "Do you have to go?"

Her question took me so much by surprise that I actually answered, "Hell, we've covered just about every subject there is to talk about."

She pinned me with eyes round with incredulity. "Dave Bolt, you really are a big dumb cowboy."

I recognized my gaffe. "Oh, Lordy, I really am! I just didn't think. . . I mean, it was never my intention. . ."

"I know that," she murmured, stepping close to me and raising her face. "And that's what makes it especially nice."

But even now that the scales had dropped from my eyes, she still took me by surprise with the urgency of her kiss and the potency of her need. Her soft lips parted and her warm tongue swept the inside of my mouth. Her hips thrust up to my pelvis and her fingers gripped the back of my neck like the talons of a hawk. I had seldom seen female passivity convert so quickly and thoroughly to aggressive action, and frankly. . .

Well, frankly, I never did get my shit together, if you know what I mean. It was like drifting lazily down a quiet stream one minute, then hurtling down violent rapids the next. I didn't fight it—oh, mercy me, no, I definitely did not fight it—but neither did I quite gain control. Or putting it another way, I got on top of the girl, but not of the situation.

She led me into the bedroom, undressed, and fell heavily on her back on the bed, breathing impatiently as I stripped out of my clothes. There were no preliminaries. She pulled me atop her and shoveled her bottom up to me before I was fully ready. There were some embarrassing proddings before I finally slid fully into her, but my temporary difficulty was rectified by the passionate churning of her hips, which drew me into a ramrod of flesh on which she writhed like a snake impaled on a lance. She panted so loudly it scared me, and before I could get up a full head of steam she let out a primitive moan of ecstasy and exploded in a series of high-megaton convulsions.

It took her five minutes to catch her breath. "My God, I didn't realize how much. . . what a long time it's been."

"I'd reckon so," I said.

"Would you mind getting me a cigarette? They're in my purse on the hall table."

I reluctantly disembarked from her warm perspiration-moist body and did her bidding. When I returned, she lay diagonally across her ornate brass bed, legs parted as I'd left them, breasts stretched taut, ruby nipples still erect. She wasn't panting any more, but still breathed deeply, occasionally squirming as if from some fugitive twinge of pleasure.

She looked at me apologetically. "I guess you didn't. . .?"

"No, but that's all right," I said. This wasn't strictly true. I was rather painfully tumid and felt slightly foolish standing at the foot of the bed with my supercargo awkwardly swinging in the breeze.

She lit up and hissed a narrow stream of blue smoke into the thin blade of light from the living room that sliced the darkness over her bed. I sat down beside her, wanting to caress her tenderly but afraid of aggravating my condition with the excitement of touching her. I forced my mind to dwell on non-sexual images, food and baseball, player trades and the national economy, and after a minute I'd returned to what in ballet they call First Position. It hurt only a little.

"Where do you go from here?" she asked.

"I don't know. I never did book myself into a hotel."

She poked me playfully. "That's not what I meant. But as long as you've mentioned it, you'll stay here, of course."

"That's very kind of you."

"Kind?" She sighed exasperatedly. "Do all Texans talk as gallantly as you?"

"I doubt it. I'm the last of a dying breed."

"What I meant was, where do you go from Pittsburgh?"

"South. Texas, maybe Florida and Arizona. I have that little list I told you about, plus a few other people the commissioner wants me to talk to. And what about you? You said you had some ideas about who beat up Willie."

"I do."

"You're not inclined to talk about them. Why?"

"It's—well, just a wild theory."

"If that's all it was, you'd tell it to me."

She smiled. "Yes. So why don't you let it go at that?"

"Because I'm afraid you're going to get yourself in trouble, and maybe hurt. Anyone who went to the lengths they went to to stop Willie isn't going to pull any punches to protect himself from snoopy young ladies. The thought of so much as a bruise on this alabaster flesh makes me want to weep," I said, venturing a sweep of my fingertips across her belly.

She shuddered and covered my hand. "Thanks for caring."

"Do you think you're so hard to care about?"

"Sometimes I think I'm horrid."

"I find you anything but."

"You've known me only half a day."

"And half a night, don't forget that."

She rolled close to me and put her hand on my chest. "I'm afraid it wasn't very satisfying for you."

"There's half a night left—don't forget that, either."

Her hand glided down my chest and slid like a velvet glove over my thighs. The effect was electrifying. "It would be hard to forget," she whispered.

"Let's make it even harder."

She looked up at me and laughed. Then the laughter faded and her eyes glazed as she found me and brought me rapidly to readiness.

This time we took it real slow.

Chapter VI

• • • •

As the little truck towed our jet backwards out of the gate, I glimpsed Fiona standing behind a plate glass window in the lounge, seeking a last glimpse of me. She looked tired and a little forlorn. I'd seen the look before, of a woman wondering if a beautiful one-night stand would develop into something lasting or die on the vine as so many others had, plunging her back into loneliness. I wondered about it myself. I didn't regard her as a one-night woman. As we'd whispered together in the quiet darkness of early morning, I'd found a depth of beauty and intelligence in her that cried out for deeper exploration. I'd promised her my love wouldn't end with the dawn.

But sex is a cruel, deceitful bitch and extracts promises from us in the throes of ecstasy that we can't always keep. For all I knew, she'd leave me in the lurch when the throbbing between her thighs ceased and reality closed over the memory like the heavy door of a vault. I'd been as much victimized by one-night stands as I'd victimized others. Even as the jets whined, propelling my taxiing plane away from the terminal, I could feel the out-of-sight, out-of-mind syndrome wedging itself between us.

A good breakfast plus two extra cups of coffee followed by a catnap took the edge off my funk and after throwing some water on my face in the lavatory aft, I set Fiona in my mental file marked Follow Up and turned my thoughts from the past to the future, from the chill and grimy cities of the North to the warmth and clean spaciousness of the South. With every mile logged southward, my spirits rose and I could almost tangibly feel Texas looming before the prow of the airship like some great soft, comfortable childhood bed to which one returns. The mere prospect of returning hyped me like an amphetamine; the tasks before me pumped me full of the lust of challenge. I wouldn't swear to it but my cares seemed to drop away precisely at the moment the plane crossed the Mason-Dixon Line and I grew restless for action. I spent the last half-hour of the flight pacing the rear of the cabin and pestering the stewardesses.

We alighted in Houston shortly before noon. A muggy haze hung over the city, faintly reeking of kerosene and crude oil, and I laughed at my romantic conception of a Texas that had all but gone out of existence twenty-five years ago. But I still carried it in my heart as fresh as it was when I was a kid.

I took a taxi into Houston, directing the driver to the Galleria, the stunning new shopping mall and office center where Sam Metcalf, deposed by the Players Association in the furor over Willie's beating, had returned to private law practice. His firm was a multi-named affair in a tall office building next to the Houston Oaks, with a gargantuan office decorated in what passes for good taste in those parts, cowhide upholstery, longhorn sculpture, metal lamps whose bases are cunningly designed to look like oil rigs, a large shag rug shaped like the state of Texas. At one time I'd have been impressed but I guess I've lived too long in New York; it was pure hokum.

The receptionist, a long-stemmed beauty in a tight silk blouse, passed me right through to Sam's office, where I found him stooped over cartons of law books, placing them precisely on the dark walnut shelves that constituted one solid wall of his office. When he straightened to shake my hand, he seemed oddly smaller than I'd remembered from my dealings with him when he was ramrod of the Players Association. His face had more creases, too, and his hair was grayer. His blue eyes had a film over them, the flesh gathered in wrinkled folds around his collar and string tie, and his handshake was devoid of energy. It was painfully clear that he'd taken a terrible whipping from the ballplayers. I'd known Sam for many years and remembered what a figure he'd cut in the Texas state legislature when he defended a movement to organize cotton workers, a decidedly unpopular thing to do. This simply wasn't the same man.

Without asking, he went to the bar and fixed two bourbons and branch water. I grinned. "Now I know I'm home," I said, saluting him with my glass.

"I know what you mean, Dave. The dearth of branch water in New York was undeniably the most difficult aspect of my job. Good Christ, those Yankees are barbarians! They'll take their water from the tap. Bourbon and chlorine, fluorine, bacilli, marine worms, piss and shit—God only knows what was in that water. My mouth is just beginning to taste sweet for the first time in two years. Another month of pure Texas branch water and I'll be almost glad those folks gave me the boot."

He tried to conceal his bitterness behind garrulous banter but it didn't fool either of us. He collapsed heavily into the leather chair behind his desk and shook his head. "God, they pulled the rug out from under me, those sonsofbitches. I mean, they really fucked me for fair, Dave."

"They were scared, the players were, Sam. People do funny things when they're scared."

"I've seen frightened cattle behave with better sense than those stampeding ballplayers," he muttered.

"It's not your fault. You just happened to get in their way."

"I had such a good thing going, such a sweet deal lined up for them, and those fools threw it away. If they'd held out, if they hadn't panicked, we could have emerged in the most powerful position athletes have ever found themselves in." He looked at me dolefully. "Couldn't you have reined your client in?" He didn't seem to have enough energy to be angry about it.

"I reasoned with Willie, Sam. I even warned him. He knew his action would stir up a storm. He also knew it could be personally dangerous. In the end, it was his decision. I hope you won't hold it against me."

He shrugged wearily. He was too drained to hold anything against anyone. "I guess if it hadn't been Willie, it would have been somebody else. A lot of the players were beginning to weaken."

"Most likely."

He drained his glass and ruminated on an ice cube, then looked up hard. "I hope you don't hold anything against me."

I felt he would speak without prompting and I said nothing.

He tapped a little pile of newspaper clippings on his otherwise clean desk. "I mean, you don't believe any of this stuff, do you?"

He was alluding to insinuations in the press that he had known about, or even devised, the plan for Willie's "accident."

"Shit no, Sam," I said. And I meant it.

That didn't stop Sam from launching into an exoneration of himself. "Jesus, Dave, I may be hard-liner but I'd no more consider violence than I'd consider swimming the Brazos in a lead bathing suit. Willie Hesketh was a scab and he should have been made an example of. But not that way. There are lots of other ways the players could have punished him, silent treatment. . . oh, hell, I don't have to tell you." He shuffled the clippings again and tossed them down angrily on his desk. "The shit they'll print when they're hard up for a story, these sportswriters." He fixed himself another drink. I declined a second for myself. Abruptly Sam plopped into his seat and slammed his glass down on his desktop. "A man would have to be insane!"

"Come again?"

"A man would have to be insane to do something that would bring all that heat down on himself. I'm talking about me, now. I'd have had to be clear out of my calabaza to condone any scheme to stop Willie by force. But who in Sam Hill do you think everyone would think of first? Me!"

"You, or Pinky Ryan."

He blanched, and his brow furrowed like the slats of a venetian blind. "What do you know about Pinky Ryan?"

"That you signed a secret agreement with him."

"Who told you?"

"The commissioner has big ears."

He grabbed the bourbon bottle and poured himself three inches of pure alcohol. "I suppose that'll hit the papers next. Oh, what a stink it's gonna make when it does. With half of Congress calling for an investigation. . ."

"We're trying to hold the lid on as long as we can. It'll just complicate things if the press gets hold of it."

"Complicate things? It could be the next Watergate, for the love of Mike."

"Well, then, what about Pinky Ryan? What about the Federation of Skilled Workers? What about that secret agreement?"

His eyes had reddened and become watery and his voice slurred with the spreading effect of Kentucky's best but he was still cogent. "Dave, how long have you known me?"

"We go back quite a ways, Sam."

"And you know I'm not capable of pulling a stunt like that, right?"

"I already said so."

"Well, I've known Pinky Ryan just as long, if not longer. And I swear to you, by all that is holy, that that man is no more capable of it than I am. He'd sooner cut his hands off at the wrists. Christ, if he wore a frock, he'd be a fucking saint."

"Then you think it was ballplayers?"

"Of course it was ballplayers. You know how hot some of them were. Hell, even some of the moderates saw red when they read Willie's announcement in the papers."

I reached into my blazer pocket and handed Sam the list of names the commissioner had given me. He peered at it, rubbed his eyes, and groped in his desk drawer for his glasses. "Sam," I said, "if it was ballplayers, it's likely to be one of the names on that paper."

"How do you reckon that?"

"Because we happen to know that Willie got a piece of one of the men who beat him up. In fact, Willie is certain he put the guy's eye out."

He looked at me. "I still don't understand how you've narrowed it down to. . . ah, of course. It's got to be a player who hasn't shown up for spring training yet."

"Right."

I sat chewing on a piece of ice and admiring the Houston skyline while Metcalf went over the list. Fiona strayed into my mind, the image of her milky body stretched over that brass bed like the lady in Bob Dylan's famous song. Sam said something and I had to ask him to repeat it.

"I said, you can eliminate Bobby Christopher and Vinny Ariana. I heard they showed up in their respective camps day before yesterday."

"Okay."

"And Breitz, Jacoby, Cruz—you can pretty much eliminate them, too."

"Why's that?"

"Because they either opposed the strike or didn't care one way or the other. If they haven't shown up in camp yet, I'm sure it's because their cars have broken down or they're shacked up with broads or haven't heard the strike is over or something equally dumb." He tapped the list with his index finger as he went over it again. "And you can knock off Bicks, Reifheimer, and McMull. They haven't an angry bone in their bodies."

"Who would you say are the likelier candidates, Sam?"

He pursed his lips thoughtfully. "Well, there's no doubt who I'd put at the top of the list."

"Buddy Gilpin?"

"Uh-huh." Gilpin was, of course, the president of the Players Association. Like Sam, he'd had the rug pulled out from under him when the players voted to go back to work. "Talk about radicals! Buddy Gilpin makes Lenin look like Gene Autry. Jesus, there's a case of politics making strange bedfellows if I ever saw one. Under any other circumstances, I'd no sooner have Buddy Gilpin for an ally than a cotton-mouth moccasin. But in his own crazy way, he did more to hold the players together than anyone I can think of."

"How far do you think he'd go to do that?"

"I just don't know. We're not talking about shades of emotion, Dave. We're talking about a quantum leap from strong feelings to murderous ones. Does anybody know if a man is capable of such a thing?"

"Why didn't Buddy show up at the emergency meeting of the players' reps?"

"He was boycotting it—I thought everybody knew that. He felt the players were about to stampede and his gesture was like planting his spurs in the ground and refusing to go along."

"Couldn't he have had another reason entirely?"

"Like what?"

"Like he'd lost an eye a couple of nights before?"

Sam held his palms up. "Your guess is as good as mine. Probably better. Anyway, I'd definitely start with Gilpin if I were you. Where does he live, again? Some jerkwater town in Louisiana."

"I've got all that information. But now tell me something else, Sam. What do you think of the notion that the men who beat Willie up were hired by an owner?"

He looked at me candidly, showing no surprise, just that overwhelming tiredness and sadness. "Dave, when you've been as closely associated with unionism as I've been, you see a lot of things. If you know anything about the movement, you know that its history is rife with examples of perfidy by management. In fact, there are precedents for exactly the kind of thing you're talking about." He went to a row of buff and red legal books on a low shelf, pulled one down, and began thumbing through it. "In 1931, for instance, there was a situation in a railroad strike—"

I raised my hand. "I'll take your word for it, Sam."

He shut the book and thrust it back between its companion volumes. "Yes, it could very well have been an owner."

"Any idea which one?"

"Yes," he said.

The word fell loudly like a shot put dropped on a wooden floor. Sam was given to running off at the mouth. When he uttered a one-syllable answer, you knew it must hold a special significance. It came as such a shock I almost didn't know what to say.

Sam himself looked a little bewildered as if the word had popped out of his throat without his volition. His mouth opened and closed wordlessly like a fish's. "What did the man say to you, Sam?" I asked quietly. "Did he say he'd stop at nothing to break the strike?"

"Men say a lot of things they don't mean in the heat of a quarrel."

"They also do things they wouldn't dream of in the heat of a quarrel. Who was it, Sam?"

He breathed the name so softly it was almost inaudible. "Ruby Swanson."

"Ruby?" I flashed on the paunchy, flamboyant Nebraskan, owner of the Omaha Honchos, formerly the San Diego Padres. Swanson had made a pile in the trucking business and brought the ailing Padres to Nebraska, fulfilling a lifelong dream. Unfortunately, he'd made the same mistake so many other parvenus make in their eagerness to own ball clubs; he'd plunked his team down in what the television networks call a low-density market, meaning not enough viewers for sponsors to expose their products to. But viewers aside, there weren't enough fans to fill the back seat of a Toyota and Swanson's first year had been a fiasco. Yet he'd determined to hold on yet another year, which in my book takes the prize for stubbornness, stupidity, or both. But he owned two clients of mine, so he couldn't be completely stupid.

He was known as a blusterer and a bully, which is why I was surprised to hear Sam mention him as a prospect for suspicion. And I said as much to Sam.

"That's just it, Dave. You'd expect Ruby to rant and rave, right? But the way he said it, kind of flat out, in the same tone of voice I'm using with you—it sent chills down my back."

"What exactly did he say? What were his precise words?"

Sam scratched his nose to invoke memory. "He said something like, 'I'll break this strike, you'll see.' I think those were his words. I said, 'How're you gonna do that, Ruby?' And he said, 'By whatever means are necessary.' I wish I could reproduce the. . . the deadliness in his voice and that look in his eyes, eerie and cruel, like some latter-day Rasputin."

"The Honchos train somewhere in Texas, don't they? Wichita Falls or someplace?"

"Lubbock."

I exhaled heavily. I was glad to be back in Texas, sure enough, but I reckoned I'd be good and tired of it by the time I wrapped up this one—and at the rate I was making progress, I figured that to be sometime around the turn of the century. The twenty-third century.

Chapter VII

• • • •

I was ravenous for Mexican food and lunched alone in a little joint off Crockett called El Imperator. The pleasure was so exquisite it brought tears to my eyes. Or maybe it was the jalapeños, the little Mexican peppers that are pickled in molten lava. New York City had for some reason witnessed an explosion of Mexican restaurants of late, but except for one or two, their food was no more authentic than the made-in-Brooklyn serapes and straw hats that decorated their phony adobe walls. My daddy used to say, if you don't find at least one dead cockroach in your chili it ain't Meskin food, two live ones and you know it's Meskin for a true fact. My own criterion is whether the chili sears every mucous membrane in your cranial cavity and this did. Roy Lescade says his cousin Ernie struck oil dropping jalapeños down a gopher hole outside of Kilgore.

I flooded my throat with cold Mexican beer and traced imaginary lines on the gaudy map of Texas that served as a paper placemat. I was trying to line up an efficient itinerary but no matter which way I set it up, I'd have to do a lot of traveling and doubling back to see all the people I wanted to see: Buddy

Gilpin in Louisiana, Ruby Swanson in Lubbock, my mom and
my ex-wife and my kid up in Fort Worth, and, oh yes, if I had
a chance, I'd promised Roy Lescade's friend Bonnie I'd visit
her boyfriend in the state prison over at Bristow.

My first priority was Buddy Gilpin, who lived in Hackberry, a little town west of Lake Calcasieu forty or fifty miles
over the Sabine River border in Louisiana. I arranged for a
private plane to fly me to Orange, Texas, a half hour's flight
east from Houston, then rented a car in Orange, crossed
the bridge spanning the Sabine River, and picked up US
90 in a northeasterly direction. I found myself traversing a
scrubby, marshy flatland totally alien to my orientation of
grassy plains and I felt a bit more comfortable only when I
entered an oilfield in Vinton, Louisiana. Oil derricks were
something I could identify with. I continued on 90 to Sul-
phur, named, not unbelievably, for huge deposits of same.
Then I hung a right on Louisiana 104 and found myself in
the midst of some pretty farmland that soon gave way to
marshy meadows on which I glimpsed wild Creole ponies
grazing. Here and there a chênière, an oak-covered ridge,
broke up the monotony. I crossed Bayou Choupique, fer-
ried across the Intracoastal Waterway at Port Ellender, and
pulled into Hackberry ten minutes later.

Hackberry wasn't exactly a jerkwater town, as Sam Metcalf had designated it, but neither was it Eden. Its population
was twenty-five or so, supported by trade from the East and
West Hackberry oil fields, and aside from a mock-planta-
tion-style hotel surrounded by mossy oaks, there was nothing
agreeable about the tiny cluster of houses and stores on the
town's main—and only—street. There was an unpleasant
odor in the air of smoked fish and Louisiana crude.

I parked the car, trotted up the stairs of the hotel,
crossed the wooden verandah that girdled it, and plunged

into the cool darkness of the lobby. A short, owlish man was working an old-fashioned mechanical adding machine at the front desk and took his time looking up at me. "Yes?"

"Does Buddy Gilpin live hereabouts?"

His chin jerked up suddenly, and he blinked. "Uh, you might say that."

"Where would I find him?"

"Oh, he's usually out crabbing or fishing around this time. You'd never find him by yourself. But he usually shows up here at the bar about now, if you want to wait." He twiddled nervously with the knob of his adding machine. "Who am I supposed to say is asking for him?"

"Tell him Mr. Bolt."

"Will he know who you are?"

"Are you his secretary, or what?" I growled.

"Oh no, no, no," he tittered. He seemed ill at ease, almost excited. I wondered if Gilpin had posted sentries around the town to warn him if strangers came looking for him. If so, this clown filled the bill.

"The bar is. . .?"

"That way," the clerk said with a pointed index finger. "I'll tell Mr. Gilpin you're here when he comes in."

I started for the bar, then turned back. "By the way, how's his eye?"

The clerk frowned. "His eye?"

"Wasn't there something wrong with his eye?"

"I wouldn't know, sir. He always wears dark glasses, far as I know."

I crossed the genteel lobby to the bar, a wonderfully nostalgic paneled room with slow-turning ceiling fans and an etched mirror of turn-of-the-century vintage. There were two or three old-timers in grease-stained coveralls yarning about oil wells they'd brought in. A black bartender right out of Central Casting was polishing the oak bar to a brilliant sheen.

The drink I nursed while waiting for Buddy Gilpin did little to relieve a growing anxiety in the pit of my stomach. I did some reviewing and came up perplexed. Buddy Gilpin, the sparkplug of the Players Association, suddenly makes himself scarce after Willie's beating. He's not even present for the critical emergency meeting where only his fiery eloquence, perhaps, can reverse the tide in favor of returning to camp. Oh sure, he sends this eloquent telegram but what weight does that carry against a personal appearance at a conclave that may well decide the future of baseball? He claims he's boycotting in protest against the railroading of panicky players. But can I buy that? Isn't his real reason for shunning camp the fact that he lost his eye in the fray with Willie Hesketh?

I finished my drink and looked at my watch, got up and went back to the desk clerk. His distress to see me manifested itself in a smarmy smile. "Ah, I was just coming to find you, Mr. Bolt. Mr. Gilpin called—to ask if there were any messages. I told him you were here. He said you could find him on Lake Calcasieu, fishing."

I leaned over the desk angrily. The clerk shrank like a varmint in the shadow of a plummeting eagle. "He called you, huh?"

"Uh. . . uh. . . yes. Yes."

"You're sure you didn't call him?" I wrapped his tie around my hand and drew his face close to mine. His eyes bulged and his face purpled. I eyeballed him for a minute until he started to make rasping sounds. I released him and he fell heavily onto his stool. "Where on Lake Calcasieu? It's a big lake."

"Bayou Cheval," he gurgled, rubbing his throat and sucking in air. He gave me specific directions and I left the hotel and got into my car. Well, now the game got interesting. Gilpin had been alerted and was undoubtedly isolating himself to get the upper hand in a one-on-one contest. It now dawned on me that we weren't talking about hopscotch; the man I sought was dangerous and lethal and probably armed with ordnance considerably heavier than a baseball bat. Against which I could pit—what? I had (if Hertz had done its job right) a tire iron in the trunk if I wanted to use it. I had a second thought about bearing a weapon, which might only provoke violence. Then I had a third thought that if Buddy Gilpin was my man, my presence would be provocation enough. I decided to carry the tire iron.

At the end of the main street, I turned left and followed a narrow road that tunneled beneath bowers of willows and moss-bearded oaks and an even higher canopy of bamboo. The setting sun flashed through the leafy interstices like the mirrored ball of a discotheque. I heard a pair of boat-tailed grackles challenging each other and glimpsed some sparrows, red-winged blackbirds, and marsh wrens. Tree swallows were starting to swarm for insects at sundown.

My heart was pounding heavily in my chest. Just what the hell was Gilpin's game, anyway? Was he setting me up for an ambush? Ignoring me? Or was he just, for crying out loud, fishing?

The heavy foliage dropped away for a man-made clearing providing for a boat dock and the lovely enormity of Lake Calcasieu opened up before me, a stretch of forest green water fringed by cypresses, willows, and oleander. On the far side, I could see, on or near the shore, an ornithologist's dream come true, herons and egrets and ducks and plovers swimming, swarming, and swooping. The only other sound was the hoot of an oil tanker somewhere up around the deep-water port of Lake Charles to the north-east but soon the bullfrogs would launch their nocturnal cacophony. Jesus, how I wished I'd come here to fish—this was God's gift to the angler.

But I had bigger fish to fry, pardon the pun. I got out of the car, removed the tire iron from the trunk, and walked down a slight incline to the boat dock. Three or four row-boats and pirogues bobbed on the lapping ripples beside the dock. I looked around. There was nobody there, at least that I could see. I looked across the lake, to my right, where the clerk had told me was the inlet, Bayou Cheval, in which I'd find Gilpin. I thought I made out a slight indentation but saw nothing else in the rapidly fading light.

I stood uncertainly over the boats, hung up momentarily by my compunctions about stealing until I resolved them by calling it borrowing. I selected a slim pirogue that was more canoe than rowboat and removed a paddle from a rack at the end of the dock. I looked over my shoulder. The sun had sunk below the treetops. Darkness would descend fast. I should move quickly. I was at enough of a disadvantage without also having to grope my way around a pitch-black bayou looking for a potential murderer.

I set my tire iron and paddle into the pirogue and stepped into it, unhitched the painter, and began paddling in the direction of the cove about a mile to the south. I had to stop every four strokes to swat the mosquitoes and no-see-ums that exploded out of the marsh undaunted by the squadrons of swallows that preyed on them.

After ten minutes, the bayou, shaped like a horse's head (hence its name), loomed into view, a lily-choked inlet circumscribed by cypresses and tupelos. The rubbery lily leaves drubbed the bottom of my boat and I withdrew my paddle to look and listen. At first, I saw nothing but the unrelieved monotony of the shoreline silhouetted against the purple dusk. Then I glimpsed the low profile of a rowboat beached on a large brake, or maybe it was an island, dead ahead. I muscled my paddle into the water and glided up to the shore. The boat was beached on an exposed tree root. I pulled up beside it, stepped out, and pulled my pirogue halfway out of the water. Then I reached into it and removed the tire iron.

The open shore extended only a few yards from the water. Then I confronted thick, whippy marsh grass and bulrushes seven feet tall. A few yards beyond that, those ubiquitous cypresses. My imagination conjured a dozen terrible things that could happen to me if I ventured forward, ranging from getting lost to drowning to stepping on a water moccasin to getting shot, and the odd thing is, none of these were paranoid fantasies—they really could happen to me! I've never considered myself a coward but courage is relative and must be set in its proper context. I've never hesitated to run a shallow slant pattern even though I knew I'd be clotheslined by a safety, barreled by a linebacker, and piled on by a cornerback the instant I caught the pass. But would I walk five yards into swampy terra incognita harboring a man who was aiming to bushwhack me?

Well, the answer is yes. Not unequivocally yes, mind you—just bare-minimum yes. I knew I was playing Gilpin's game and I hated myself for it. Yet I was drawn magnetically to a confrontation or maybe pushed is a better word, pushed by my obligation to Willie Hesketh and the commissioner and Sam Metcalf and Fiona and all the decent people who'd been befouled by that terrible deed on a Florida road. I had to know the truth, had to confront Buddy Gilpin, had to look him in the eyes. Or eye.

I paused, entered the chest-high grass, then paused again to listen and adjust my senses to the dark strangeness. Then

I continued. My handsome stitched leather boots made to order by Tony Lama of El Paso squished through soggy peat and anyone who's ever paid two hundred dollars for a pair of boots knows what that can do to a man's insides. I stalked my prey in the darkness like a raccoon, the hairs on my scalp tingling like antennae as I sensed his presence in the vicinity.

My senses were right. But that did me no good. The foliage on my right seemed to explode as a heavy, dull object glanced off my wrist and rammed into my diaphragm. Even as the wind left my lungs on the wings of a groan, I brought the tire iron around in a blind swing at my assailant. I struck wood so hard my hands tingled. I guessed it to be an oar. After my thrust, he pushed the shank of the oar out at my face with both hands, clipping me on the jaw. I still hadn't caught my breath and sank into the spongy peat. The man, cursing, came down on my back with both knees. Applying the oar to the back of my neck, he thrust my face into the mush. He was tremendously strong and it was all I could do to turn my face to one side to keep from being suffocated. Had he wanted to, he probably could have broken my neck at that moment or suffocated me, but he just leaned heavily on top of me, breathing hard. He took the tire iron out of my hands and threw it away.

"Okay, motherfucker, who are you and what's your game?" It was Gilpin. I recognized the voice.

"Mff," I replied, "Cliff groof." The muddy moss in my mouth did very little for elocution.

He relaxed the pressure a little and got to his feet, strad-dling my back. "All right, mister, turn over re-e-e-al slow."

I rolled beneath the oar until I was on my back. He pressed the heavy wooden shaft against my gullet. My throat was pie dough and the oar a rolling pin. Against the now black, rapidly clouding sky I saw the outline of a massive head with a medusa tangle of hair.

"Now, suppose we run it through again. Who are you?"

"Dave Bolt," I rasped.

"Who sent you?"

That was bad luck. He didn't recognize my name. "I'm the agent," I explained as coherently as a three-inch shaft of lumber propped against my adam's apple permitted. "I'm Willie Hesketh's agent."

What made me think this would make him automatically release me, I can't imagine. I realized at once that he must believe I'd come to avenge Willie.

"I came to ask you some questions," I said, straining my eyes in the darkness for a clear look at his eyes. I could make out a pair of faint white glimmers but that told me nothing. "That's all, just questions," I emphasized.

"Sure. You come to kill me."

"If I'd come to kill you, do you think I'd be armed with nothing more than a tire iron?"

He thought about that. "Ask your questions."

"How can I ask 'em with this on my throat, asshole?"

I could feel him glaring at me. "A turd in your position can't afford to call a man in mine an asshole." I felt the pressure on my gullet ease slightly as if he'd taken a hand off the oar momentarily. "Can you see in the dark, Bolt?"

"A little."

"Then maybe you can make out what I got here." I glimpsed an object about a foot long that glinted silver in the faint background light of the cloudy Louisiana night. "I'll give you a hint. It can gut a tarpon in fifteen seconds flat. A man takes maybe a few seconds less. I'll just hold it here against your dick while we have a nice chat."

He removed the oar from my throat and set it down prudently out of my reach. Then I felt the cold steel of his fishing knife through the fabric of my pants. "Okay," he said, "ask your questions."

I wanted to ask him how many eyes he had, but I figured that was the fastest way for me to achieve eunuch status. "Why aren't you back in training camp?"

"Because nobody's invited me, for one thing. My contract expired last year and Mr. Bowles and the other folks in the Braves' front office don't seem to be in a screaming rush to renew it."

"Because of your role in the strike?"

"For sure. I'm a burr in the britches of major league baseball. You've seen what happens even to the quiet players' reps—half of 'em get traded away. Imagine what they're gonna do to a nuisance like me? I'll be lucky if the Little League picks me up on waivers." He grunted. "But you know what? Even if they offered me a million-dollar contract, I wouldn't fall in with those chickenshit pukes."

"You mean, the other ballplayers?"

He grunted again in the affirmative. "They ain't one amongst 'em what has the balls of a shithouse mouse. They've been so corrupted by the consumer ethos and trapped in the snares of the capitalist dialectic—"

"Buddy, why don't you cut the bullshit?" I snapped.

He hissed like an iguana and I felt the knife-blade twitch against my crown jewels. "You are living dangerously, my friend."

"You're hiding out, Buddy."

He laughed. It was a sound I cared for very little. "Hiding out? Why would I do that?"

"Because you did the number on Willie Hesketh."

My balls tingled in anticipation of the knifeblade's coup de grâce, but Buddy hung fire. "You know where I was the morning of Willie's so-called accident? I was in Parcperdue, Louisiana, eating hominy casserole and vinegar pie with my wife, my mama, my papa, my sisters and brothers, and half the townfolk including the deputy sheriff, Bobby-Don Keechie. Now, if you'd like to check that story out, you're perfectly welcome."

"Supposing that's true, tell me again why you're hiding out."

"You say I'm hidin' out. I ain't never said it. I'm just gone fishin'."

"If you're just fishing, what are you doing setting up a Distant Early Warning system back in Hackberry? Why'd you run off when that hotel clerk told you I was in town? How come I had to flush you out of the marsh like a swamp turkey? Who are you expecting, Buddy?"

The long silence before he answered was filled only by the honking of a nearby bullfrog and the distant hoot of another tanker. "Who ain't I?" he finally said. "Half the country suspects I did the job on Willie. I'm expecting everyone and anyone, from the FBI to union torpedoes to Willie Hesketh's kid brother—or even his agent. I don't know who might come lookin' for me but until they find out who worked Willie over, I'm gonna be scarcer than a whoopin' crane. And if you think an oar and a knife are all I got to defend myself with. . . mister, you are one lucky dude I didn't hit you with what I wanted to hit you with. You'd have a buckshot hole in you big enough to pass a telephone pole through—sideways!"

"I guess this is my lucky day," I said. My stomach and jaw would be sore for a week. "Listen, would you mind letting me get up? I'm soaked to the skin and I'm beginning to stink like a swamp rat."

He sighed, then pushed off me with a groan. "Yeah, get up." He grabbed my wrist and pulled me to my feet, then snapped a flashlight in my eyes. "I'm still covering you, Bolt. You do anything you're not supposed to and I'll make catfish bait out of your heart."

I turned away from the glare. I'd still not had a good look at his eyes, and at this rate, I wasn't going to get one. Then I had an inspiration. "You got a cigarette?"

"Yeah." I waited a second, then a pack of Winstons and a book of matches spun out of the darkness and into the cone of light and fell at my feet. I lit a cigarette and returned the pack. He shifted the flashlight under his armpit and held it on me while he tapped a cigarette out of the pack. Then the light dipped as he struck a match and raised it to his cigarette. I gazed intently at his face as the orange glow flickering in his cupped palm illuminated his face, a strong, broad face with swarthy complexion but it was the eyes I was interested in. By this time I was pretty sure I'd been wrong about him, but I had to be absolutely certain.

He had as many good eyes as I had.

Of course, that didn't necessarily rule him out. There were three men besides the one who lost an eye on the raiding party in Florida and Buddy could have been one of those. But my instincts touted me off Buddy, touted me off baseball players as suspects. That solution was just too pat, had been pat right from the start.

I plumped down heavily on a tree stump.

"Buddy, who do you think took a bat to Willie?"

"There's no doubt in my mind," he said with a hiss of smoke. "The owners are behind it. I'll bet that surprises you, huh?"

"No, I'm familiar with that theory."

"It's a beautiful ploy. Make it look like the players did it so as to force them to come to terms. It's just the kind of rotten trick you might expect from those exploitive pigs." He smoked quietly for a minute. "You ever go frogging?"

"Sure."

"Bet you never did it this way." He shined his flashlight into a tangle of cypress roots about ten yards away. The beam picked out the glassy orange of a huge pair of eyes, so big that if I'd seen them in a tree I'd have thought they belonged to an owl. "We got whoppers down here," he said as he picked up the oar and stalked the creature, which looked transfixed into the white beam. Bearing the oar in the crook of his arm, he crept to within two feet of the frog, which glup-glupped obliviously. He then drew the oar away, fulcrumming it in the bend of his elbow, and swung it around in a gray blur, catching the frog full with the paddle part and knocking him ten yards away. Laughing like a hyena, Buddy followed the frog's trajectory through the air with his flashlight. I felt sick.

He shined the light back on me and I wondered if he was planning to tee off on my head next. But all he did was speak quietly. "Don't think I wouldn't have loved to do that to Willie Hesketh, that miserable puke. He personally destroyed our strike with his selfishness."

"He only wanted to play baseball," I said, remembering my last talk with him.

"Play baseball! What the hell does that matter when you set it beside the goal of liberation of the downtrodden, exploited—"

"Buddy," I interrupted, "if it's all the same to you, I'm going to paddle back to Hackberry and get some sleep."

He laughed bitterly. "You're caught up in the ethos, too, aren't you?"

"Tell it to the frogs," I said plodding out of the grass in the direction of my boat.

Chapter VIII

· · · ·

I rose before dawn next morning after a sleepless night in a stuffy room on the top floor of the Hackberry Arms. My ribs and jaw throbbed from Buddy Gilpin's artful application of the oar and I'd tossed in clammy sheets for hours. In spite of my bone-weariness, my mind wouldn't let me find refuge in slumber. I sought a glimmer of light beneath the bushel of stories people had been handing me the last couple of days. Pinky Ryan said one thing, Sam Metcalf another, and Buddy Gilpin still another. Now suspicion shifted to Ruby Swanson, owner of the Omaha Honchos but if the pattern held, he'd have a story just as good as the others. I didn't know whether to believe all of them, some of them, or none of them.

I paid my bill and took off without a shave or a cup of coffee, which means I was desperate to leave. I had to admit the marshland at that hour, wreathed in vapor, took on an eerie loveliness. An occasional chênière with its ghostly, moss-festooned oaks offered oasis-like solidity in a world that seemed composed of floating clods of earth.

I had to conclude that Thomas Jefferson must have been a little deranged when he bought the Louisiana Territory.

I crossed the Sabine back into Orange, Texas, filling my lungs with fresh cool air spiced with salt borne off the Gulf of Mexico by a southerly breeze. I stopped for breakfast at a gleaming diner and ducked into the men's room with my razor for a shave while waiting for my order. Three cups of coffee, huevos rancheros, sausages, and grits put me back among the living.

I'd figured to proceed to Lubbock, where Ruby Swanson's Honchos had their camp, but a phone call ascertained that the Honchos were in Tucson for an exhibition game with the San Francisco Giants and weren't due back till tomorrow morning. That was just as well since Lubbock was way to hell and gone in the northwest corner of the state and there were a couple of stops I wanted to make nearer to where I was. For one thing, there was the State Prison at Bristow where I had to go see this Lonnie Raintree as a favor to my buddy Roy. From there, I figured to go to Fort Worth to see my mom, my ex-wife, and our daughter. I could be in Fort Worth tonight and Lubbock tomorrow without skipping a beat.

I went to the phone and lined up this itinerary. Then I called Fiona.

The memory of our night together had by no means been tarnished by subsequent events. If anything, the lonesomeness of my chase across the comfortless desolation of southwest Louisiana had only vivified it. It was something warm to cling to as I became more and more deeply mired in the futility of my mission.

Part of what had kept me tossing all night was a growing sense of concern for her. She'd said she had a notion about who had ambushed Willie Hesketh but for reasons she wouldn't tell me, she wanted to follow them up on her own. I'd too blithely taken her reassurances that she'd be careful. The more I thought about it, the more I concluded she was either naive about the danger or indifferent to it. Neither attitude was healthy. I was now determined to exact from her a promise she'd do nothing without checking with me first.

Her office phone buzzed twice, then a switchboard girl picked up. I asked for Fiona, and she put me on hold for a minute. When the phone clicked again, the voice that greeted me was that of Pinky Ryan.

"Dave, my boy, good to hear from you!" His greeting was sunny. Too sunny. I didn't buy it from the git-go.

"I was hoping to speak to Fiona."

"Ah, yes. Well, she's out at the moment. Is there anything I can help you with?" His voice trembled as if I'd taken him by surprise.

"When do you expect her back?"

"Oh . . . ah. . . I'm not sure. She's out of town."

"On business?"

"Yes. Yes, in a manner of speaking."

"In what manner of speaking, Mr. Ryan? Has it anything to do with what we talked about?"

Some people are capable of lying as if it were second nature to them. Ryan wasn't one of them. The quaver in his voice betrayed him as did the vague and breezy way he said, "You might say that, yes."

My heart rate doubled. "Mr. Ryan, where is Fiona?"

There was a long pause, during which a vital association began pressing into my brain like some creature in the womb stirring to be born.

"Frankly, Dave, I don't know. I'd hoped to hear from her by now." There was no disguising his worry anymore.

I tried to hold my rising fear in check, but I could hear the edge in my own voice. "Do you have an idea, at least? You must have an idea." I had an idea myself, but it refused to be delivered into my consciousness. The frustration was maddening.

"Look, Dave, I'm sure everything is okay. Why don't you just give it a couple more days?"

I was practically shouting now. "Mr. Ryan, this isn't any goddamn Doris Day movie. Your own daughter may be—"

"Look, Dave," Ryan said, his voice rising to match the pitch of mine, "even if I knew where Fiona was, I want to remind you that this is our quarrel with . . . this is our quarrel, and we're going to settle it ourselves using our own means."

He hung up the phone at the precise instant the elusive association I'd been grappling with sprang into the forefront of my mind, for Ryan himself had served as midwife when he slipped and said, "This is our quarrel with. . ." Even though he'd canceled the rest of the sentence, the object of his preposition had flashed before my eyes with dazzling clarity.

Fioretta.

Somehow, I didn't yet understand in what way, Mark Fioretta, Pinky Ryan's professional enemy, was involved in the attack on Willie Hesketh.

I started to call Ryan back to confront him with it, but I dropped the phone back on its cradle halfway through dialing. Ryan would not, I was certain, take the call.

I stood in the booth, breathing hard with a combination of fright and helplessness. It was intolerable for me to leave the situation where it was, yet impossible for me to act from here, in the middle of the boonies half a nation away from Pittsburgh. My mind pored over possible remedies and produced one that was far from satisfactory but infinitely better than sitting on my duff waiting.

I called my office and asked for Dennis Whittie.

Dennis was a former Virginia Squires guard who'd dislocated his hip in an on-court collision and disappeared into that limbo to which most ex-ballplayers are consigned, except the really great ones. You go into a bar or a Colonel

Sanders chicken franchise or a stock brokerage house and if the man who waits on you is over six-foot-four, chances are he played pro basketball once upon a time. But Dennis showed up doing some undercover investigating for Niles Lauritzen, commissioner of the American Basketball Association, and we hit it off so well together I lured him away to work for me. Dennis was cool, professional, smart, and cold-blooded. He'd never let me down.

"Hey, Dave!" Another sunny greeting.

"Dennis, what are you doing right now?"

"Making paper airplanes. What do you mean, what am I doing? I'm working my ass off, as usual."

"Anything absolutely vital?"

"It depends what you call vital. I been battling Butch Van Breda Kolff on that no-cut clause in Roger Poister's contract, wrestling Brunswick on that endorsement package, and holding the tennis tour together with my fingernails. Other than that, I'm doing nothing vital."

"I mean life-and-death vital."

Dennis took the cue from my solemn tone and dropped the kidding. "What's up, Dave?"

It took a couple of minutes to bring him up to date on my recent peregrinations. I finally got to Fiona and said, "I want you to get down to Pittsburgh on the first available plane."

"And do what, exactly?"

"Find out from Pinky Ryan exactly what his daughter knows or thinks she knows. And where she's gone to or where he thinks she's gone to. And I want you to specifically press him on the question of what Mark Fioretta has to do with the case."

"Who's Mark Fioretta?"

I filled him in on the rivalry between Ryan and Fioretta.

"I don't understand why Fioretta would have Willie beat up, unless—"

Even as Dennis spoke, a theory began to solidify out of the haze. "Unless he was hoping to prevent the merger of the Players Association with Ryan's union."

"You took the words right out of my mouth."

"Put it to Ryan and see what he says and don't let him weasel out of it."

"Methods?"

"Any and all but try not to let the bruises show."

Dennis whistled softly. "Where can I reach you?"

"I'll be in Fort Worth this evening. Take these two numbers—I'll be at one of them." I gave him my mother's phone number and Nancy's, my ex.

I felt a little better when I hung up but not much. I cursed myself for not recognizing the risk Fiona was taking and a menagerie of perils paraded before my mind's eye. I hustled them into a mental coat closet and slammed the door, forcing myself to dwell on the tasks immediately ahead of me. But for the next two days, at unexpected moments, my anxieties about her would hurl themselves like caged beasts against the threshold of my imagination, almost overwhelming me with panicky fear.

I squared it with the Hertz people in Orange to let me drop my car off in Fort Worth, then started out for Bristow in Angelina County, not far from Diboll near the Neches River. Tacking west and north, I followed the Neches and the Southern Pacific railroad tracks, pulling into Bristow about eleven. The deep yellow pine forests of East Texas began to thin out up around here but they were still deep enough to give a potential escapee pause. More than a few prisoners had gotten lost in the dense woods in which the penitentiary was set like a stone chip on a huge green blanket and kissed their captors' feet when recaptured.

Like so many Southern prisons, Bristow had originally

been a Civil War stockade and most of its sprawling battlements of stained gray stone and brick dated to what was still referred to here as the War Between the States. There was a somewhat new wing on the west side if you call 1908 somewhat new. I passed through a gate guarded by a state trooper and parked my car on a cement lot outside the massive stone wall turreted with gun-towers. I had to walk the gantlet of troopers, metal detectors, and security guards and check in at a visitors' desk, where I cooled my heels fifteen minutes while my special application was processed. I'd spoken to the deputy warden on the phone from Orange but the pass he was supposed to send down never reached the visitors' clearance center. But finally, we got everything straightened out and I was conducted to the administrative area and the office of Deputy Warden Homer C. DePaw. My footsteps echoed like stones in the bleak, dimly lit corridors, and the metallic crash of gates closing and locking behind me, and the husky trustee who guided me, jarred my nerves. I've done a few days of time in county hoosegows, drunk and disorderly beefs during my two-year bout with the juice of the grape (and anything else that ferments), and they were enough to give me the screaming meemies. I was greatly relieved when we were admitted to an area that resembled, except for a rack of shotguns, automatic rifles, and tear-gas grenade launchers, a rather run-down business office.

A round-shouldered, white-haired inmate with cauliflower ears sat behind the anteroom desk. "My name is Dave Bolt," I said, handing him my pass. "I called earlier. I have an appointment with Mr. DePaw."

He squinted at me a minute, then snapped his fingers. "Dave Bolt. Dallas Cowboys, tight end, nineteen. . .?"

"Sixty-one, 'two, 'three."

"Right. Say, this is a pleasure." He pumped my hand, grinning. His teeth were yellow and chipped. "You played with Don Meredith."

"Yes."

"Helluva quarterback. Hell of a quarterback! Terrific television announcer, too. I like him more than Alex Karras on Monday night football."

"Alex is pretty good, too," I said, getting a trifle impatient.

"Do you know Cosell?"

"Personally? Yes, I know Howard."

"Ain't he somethin'?"

"He's somethin', all right. Is Mr. DePaw in or what?"

"Oh, sorry. It's not often we get a football star. I mean from the outside. We once had Burt Kilray in here, but he was doing time—seven to twelve for forgery. You know who he was, don't you? Oops, sorry." He pressed an intercom switch and announced me. A voice crackled something affirmative. "Right through there, Dave. Hey, who do you like for this year?"

"Cowboys are gonna take it all, old-timer."

"Aw, come on, you don't like Minnesota?"

"Minnesota? You got to be kidding."

He opened a gray door for me and I stepped into a small cluttered room whose walls seemed almost exclusively made out of cork for the purpose of posting bulletins, memos, wanted posters, work sheets, menus, charts, cartoons, and miscellaneous messages. There was a bank of green file cabinets to my right beneath the room's sole window, a plate of glass crusted black with the dirt of a century. I was sure it had never been washed.

Behind a scratched wooden desk sat a small, bald man wearing a brown shirt and a string tie, scribbling on a clipboard.

"Mr. DePaw? I'm Dave Bolt. Spoke to you earlier this morning."

He half got up and gave me a feeble handshake. "Yes, you're here to see Lonnie Raintree. I'm a little confused about your status, though. You say you're his agent?"

"I'm hoping to be," I said, feeling a knot in my stomach as he frowned. I never met a prison official yet who didn't put every idea in a discrete cell as if ideas were inmates to be properly classified and incarcerated.

"We really frown on anyone visiting inmates other than their attorneys and next of kin, except by application that must be reviewed by a three-man board which meets once a month. Our last meeting was two days ago, Mr. Bolt."

It was patently clear what Deputy Warden DePaw was angling for. "Gosh, sir, that really hangs me up," I groaned. "I came all the way from New York to see Lonnie and, wow, this is awful. Isn't there any way I could sort of make it worth somebody's while to, y'know, wink at these rigid restrictions and make just a teeny exception?"

He looked at me hard, a trace of a smile on his lips. "Well, I suppose an agent is pretty close to a lawyer."

"Almost the same thing exactly, Mr. DePaw. Almost the same thing exactly." I pulled out my wallet and let the corner of a fifty-dollar bill jut from it enticingly. "I was wondering, too, if I could see Lonnie privately. It's awful hard to talk to a man across a partition in one of those noisy visitors' rooms." I flicked the bill with my fingertip.

He pursed his lips. "Yes, we do that for some inmates— the good ones, that is. And Lonnie's a good one. Model prisoner, in fact. And a great favorite around here. Plus a helluva ballplayer, to boot. Major leaguer if I ever saw one. Pity he had to piss it away. Anyway, you can see him play today. We got a game against Huntsville State Prison in half an hour. After which," he said, reaching across his desk and pulling the fifty-dollar bill out of my wallet,

"I'll arrange for you to get together with him in private. Of course, by private I mean there'll have to be a guard present. That's one rule I can't break for love nor money."

"I understand. No sweat."

He scribbled some kind of instruction on a memo pad and handed it to me. "Give this to the guard in the visitors' area."

I pocketed it and DePaw rose to dismiss me. But I stayed in my seat. "I wonder if you'd mind filling me in on Lonnie," I said. "I really know very little about his case."

He shrugged and went over to his file cabinet, kneeled, and burrowed through a sardine-packed metal file. He finally pulled out a thin folder and returned to his desk. "There's very little to know, actually. Cut-and-dried all the way." He opened the folder and thumbed through the half-dozen sheets of blue, pink, and white carbon copies it contained. "On September 6th last, Ranger Lester Geary, of the Narcotics Division of the Texas Rangers Special Investigative Unit, acting on information purveyed by an anonymous informant, followed the subject—that's Lonnie—followed the subject's car on the Brownsville-Olmito road and asked the subject to pull over, which the subject did without resistance. Ranger Geary proceeded to pry the hubcaps off the subject's 1973 Plymouth Duster and discovered secreted thereunder a total of eight pounds of unprocessed marijuana in plastic bags." DePaw looked up. "Brownsville is just across the Meskin border from Matamoros, 'course."

"I know that."

"Sergeant Geary arrested the subject and subject was duly tried in the state courthouse in Brownsville on November 3rd last. He was found guilty of possession of more than half an ounce of marijuana, which is an automatic jolt of three to seven years. But he was found not guilty of possession with intent to sell." He looked up at me and said, "They convict you on that, it's mandatory life. Well, there you are, Mr. Bolt. Cut-and-dried, like I say." He tossed the file down, reached for a pipe in a gritty ashtray, and lit it with disgusting sucking noises.

"What was Lonnie's defense? What was his explanation?"

"Same as every other con's walking the yard, Mr. Bolt. Claimed he was framed. Said he's never had anything to do with dope in his life. Figured someone was out to get him. Revenge thing."

"Did he say who?"

DePaw laughed dryly. "Not by name, no. But apparently he knows who and won't tell. At least, that's what his lawyer told the judge. Didn't help Lonnie the least goddam bit, 'course. Judge Hickman said, 'You tell me who done this to you and why, son, and I'll accept a motion for retrial that very same day. But as it is, I got to do what the law says.' Broke the judge's heart, too. That's what Lonnie does to a person."

"What was he, protecting somebody? Afraid of retribution, or what?"

"Beats the shit out of me, my friend. But I want to tell you sumpin' and it's not often I say this. I really hope you can help Lonnie on account of he's one boy don't belong behind bars. Sometimes, though, I wisht he was."

"Why's that?"

"On account of he's the best sonofabitchin' third baseman I ever seen, inside stir or out. He's gonna lead us to the league champeenship—interprison thing, you know? Greatest hands I ever saw. Could run circles around Brooks Robinson. Give me that boy for five years, Bristow could retire the trophy."

"Thanks for everything, Mr. DePaw."

"You want to grab a bite to eat before the game, there's an employees' cafeteria down the corridor to your right. Meet me back here in half an hour." He pumped my hand and escorted me to the door. "Andy," he barked at the wizened trustee in the anteroom, "show Mr. Bolt where the cafeteria is and tell Howie to put his meal on my account. I suggest you avoid the chipped beef, Mr. Bolt—it's really chipped horse. But the sliced turkey ain't half bad if you smother it in giblet gravy."

Andy, the wizened old con, popped out of his chair and pounced on me when DePaw's door shut. "You really like the Cowboys this year, Dave?"

"I really do, Andy."

"You wouldn't want to put a friendly wager on that, would you?"

"What do you smoke?"

"Camels."

"Ten cartons says the Cowboys all the way."

"You're on, Dave," he grinned, clasping my hand.

Chapter IX

. . . .

Deputy Warden DePaw led me through a labyrinthine tunnel system that finally emerged on a large playing field surrounded by a barbed-wire fence dominated at each corner by a brick gun-tower. The grassless field showed the ravages of the recent football season and you could still make out the faded traces of yard markers crossing the freshly laid chalk foul lines delimiting the baseball field. Big wooden stands, accommodating maybe a thousand people altogether, sloped down to the foul lines on both the first and third base sides, and these were packed with inmates in their uniforms of blue jeans and work shirts. An occasional navy-blue uniform of a guard studded the lighter blue.

On the field, the Bristow Bullets, the home team, were warming up. Their powder blue uniforms, emblazoned with a cartoon of a convict swinging a huge bat at a ball chained to his foot, seemed dingy and worn compared to the white pinstripes of the visiting team from Huntsville, milling around their bench on the third base side.

We sat in a smaller stand of eight or ten rows behind home plate. It was designed for prison staff, trustees, and visitors and was isolated from the playing area by a high chickenwire fence. Beyond the pale, the deep green texture of the pine forest extended to the horizon. Above, a few fleecy clouds scudded in an easterly direction and the breeze took the broil out of the atmosphere.

I focused my attention on the third baseman. This was Lonnie Raintree. He was an odd-looking bird, very tall with almost spindly legs but a broad chest and wide shoulders, making him look like a man who had concentrated all his body-building efforts on his upper torso—like weightlifting sitting in a chair or something. A fringe of straw-colored hair fluffed out from under the rim of his dark peaked cap. As he tossed the ball around the horn, he seemed to move with extraordinary economy. He didn't range for the ball so much as dart at it like a striking snake, waiting until the last instant before scooping it up and pegging it. He didn't throw with his body, or even his shoulder and upper arm. His peg was a kind of snap of the forearm, everything else on his torso frozen almost as if useless. Yet the ball carried across the infield as if shot out of a gun. He used almost no energy to get the job done, yet got it done quicker than most infielders I knew. It made one wonder what the guy held in reserve. I was soon to find out.

"Ever see a game in prison before, Mr. Bolt?" my host asked.

"Can't say as I have."

"Well, then," he smiled, sucking on his pipe, "you'll prob'ly find the jokes about stealing and sending one over the wall and going into the hole funny. Anyway, with certain exceptions, like when there's a fight, baseball here is the same as anywhere else." He extended his arm and swept it from right to left. "We got a fair representation here, Mr. Bolt. Chicanos, Injuns, nigras, Anglos, even a couple Chinks. More democratic than your major leagues and more interesting by and large. The pitcher, Ernie Suarez, is doing thirty for statutory rape; the first baseman, Seth Bakey, he's doing twenty-five for armed robbery, and the second baseman, Wally Jack Wilkins, pulled twenty for homicide one. Funny thing about Texas, ain't it? The statutes against stealin' and rape are more severe than the ones against killin'. That's because life here has always been cheaper than land, women, horses, and propitty. Ah, there's our revered umpire."

"Who's that?"

"The warden, Mr. Warren Babbidge."

I chuckled. "I reckon disputes are kept to a minimum."

"You better believe it!"

Warden Babbidge strutted around home plate inspecting the batter's box. Satisfied, he hollered, "Play ball!" A baritone cheer went up from the inmates, rapidly succeeded by lusty barnyard noises as the first Huntsville batter stepped up to the plate. DePaw identified him for me by name, crime, and term. The Bristow pitcher, Suarez (thirty years for statutory rape), got him to pop to second base (Wally Jack Wilkins, twenty years for homicide one), then walked the next man. The third batter singled to center field, sending the runner to third.

That brought up the cleanup hitter, a monolithic black man with hawser-sized forearms and a neck thicker than culvert piping. "If his name isn't John Henry, it ought to be," I said to DePaw.

"His name is Oliver Hibbs and you wouldn't believe what he's in for."

"Crushing someone's head to a fine powder, I'd imagine."

"Uh-uh. Buggery. Guy's a screaming fruiter. Shrieks like a girl when you raise your voice to him. Now, what do you think of that? Just goes to show you never can tell from the looks of a man, ain't that right?"

"That's for sure."

"But he's a passing fair ballplayer and if he gets aholt of the ball, it's good-bye, Columbus."

The right-handed Hibbs took two intimidating practice swings before stepping up to the plate and assuming a wide, power-hitter's stance. He took a ball, then whacked the second pitch foul, striking it so hard it was still ascending when it cleared the left field fence. The inmates murmured with awed respect.

I looked at Lonnie. Despite the distinct possibility that Hibbs could slam the ball down his throat, Lonnie stood in for the double play, guarding the line beside the runner cautiously edging off the bag.

On the next pitch, Hibbs sent a low liner screaming into the dirt in front of Lonnie's feet. A little gout of red dust puffed into the air a yard before him, but Lonnie snapped the ball up on the short skip, merely flicking his glove out like a lizard's tongue capturing a fly. Both base runners had remained fixed in their leads waiting to see if Lonnie caught the ball in the air or off the hop. Lonnie had them dead where they stood. In one clean, catlike motion he darted his glove across the third base line to tag the runner out, pulled the ball out of his glove, and released it to second base so sharply it looked like the second baseman had yanked it with a cord. The runner at first had scarcely taken two steps toward second when the ball arrived there. That made three outs, but the second baseman chucked to first for the hell of it, beating the batter by five steps. Had there been no outs instead of one, it would have been a triple play.

DePaw nudged me so hard I almost fell off the bench. "Hah? Hah? Waddya say, Mr. Bolt? Is he somepin' or is he somepin'?"

"It's an auspicious beginning, I got to admit," I said, whistling.

Lonnie, scheduled to bat fifth, didn't come up the first inning, and in the second flied out—impressively, with a shot that took the center fielder to the fence, where a sign read 405 Feet.

The visitors got two runs in the third inning on consecutive doubles, an infield error, and a tag-up on a long out to right field, and they held the Bullets in check for four more innings. Lonnie got two more chances at third base, routine ones that he handled adeptly.

During the seventh inning stretch, with the home team behind 2-0, the inmates got a little testy and started to bay, hoot, and catcall, clapping and stamping their feet rhythmically until the stands began to shake and the bulls had to hammer their billies on the benches to subdue the disturbance. Believe me when I say there is a difference between such demonstrations in an outside ballpark and a prison one. This one was mean and ugly and suddenly the chickenwire fence separating us from this snarling rabble seemed very tenuous. Even DePaw beside me fingered his pipe nervously. But Warden Babbidge had things under control. He simply took off his mask and glared, first at the third base stands, then the first base. The decibel count dropped sharply.

"They know he's takin' names," DePaw explained. "Tain't a good idea to be on the Warden's shit-list."

The demonstration seemed to pick up the Bullets, though. A walk by their leadoff batter, followed by a Texas Leaguer behind first base, turned the inmates around. Their cheers and whistles drained the air over the field of its tension. The third batter laid down a pretty drag bunt and almost beat it out, moving the runners to second and third with one out. But unfortunately, the cleanup batter popped up to the catcher.

That brought Lonnie up.

He had an interesting stance. He kept his feet together but his knees bowed out awkwardly, like a wrangler's. And he cocked his wrists so far the bat actually touched the nape of his neck.

He took two balls, a called strike, then got fooled on a changeup, monumentally fooled, too. But he lashed so hard at it the bat appeared to bend like a fly-rod. He took a third ball inside and low—I noted his good judgment because from where I sat it looked like a strike across the knees—then crouched for the full-count pitch.

The pitcher had been throwing almost nothing but fast balls all day with an occasional off-speed pitch or knuckleball. I'd have expected him to go with his best pitch now, his fast ball, which was very fast indeed. But that's when he brought out his curve.

I have no idea how Lonnie managed to anticipate or read that pitch (DePaw later joked that the third base coach, doing time for larceny, had stolen the catcher's signals) since it was the first curve the pitcher had thrown all day. But some instinct told Lonnie that ball was going to spin in on him, for he leaned away the moment it left the pitcher's hand. He met it solidly, rocketing a shot down the third base line that didn't drop an inch on its way to the fence three hundred fifty-five feet away. The ball sproinged off the chickenwire at a weird angle beyond the glove of the center fielder racing to the left fielder's aid. Both outfielders skidded and gave chase as the ball skittered along the foot of the fence like a scared squirrel.

I'd taken my eyes off Lonnie to follow the ball and couldn't believe he'd already rounded second when I turned my gaze back to the infield. "Je-sus!" I murmured.

"Does a nine-three hundred!" DePaw shouted, pounding me on the back.

The center fielder picked the ball up with his bare hand, dug in and hurled it to the shortstop, who'd run into shallow left field for the relay. The third base coach raised his hands ordering Lonnie to stop.

Lonnie disobeyed him.

He rounded third like a careening truck whose brakes have failed. The shortstop, arm cocked to throw to third to hold Lonnie on, checked his throw and gaped for a second in disbelief. Then he pegged home as Lonnie highballed down the line. It was a perfect bullet and smacked into the catcher's mitt half a second before Lonnie. But Lonnie lowered his shoulder like a fullback and speared the catcher with his head. They tumbled across the plate in a confusion of arms and legs, and a mushroom cloud of red dust obscured the outcome. I looked at Warden Babbidge. His fist was jerking down for an Out signal, but suddenly it blurred to a halt and his flattened hands waved a reversal of his call. A moment later, the loose ball trickled across the batter's box. The roar was deafening.

Ramming the catcher is a poor idea under the best of conditions, do it in a prison game and you take your life in your hands. The catcher scrambled to his feet and leaped with both knees on top of Lonnie, pummeling him with his fists. The inmates shouted angrily and shook their fists and a few, forgetting themselves, hopped out of the stands and began to run to home plate before a dozen strident whistles brought them back to reality. I looked at the benches, expecting to see them empty for a full-scale rhubarb but agitated as the players were, milling around the protective fence in front of their bench and shouting epithets at their opponents, they kept out of the fracas. There were high penalties here for misconduct, penalties outside ballplayers didn't have to think about. Meanwhile, the warden had bent over the catcher, grabbed his hair, yanked him off Lonnie, and hollered something into his ear. The catcher glared up at the warden, grumbled something, and dropped his fists. Lonnie got to his feet, brushed the dust off his uniform, and strode back with a cocky saunter to his bench amidst the wild cheers of his teammates and the crowd.

The Bullets held Huntsville scoreless in the eighth and were in turn buffaloed in the bottom of that inning. But in the top of the ninth, with the Bullets ahead by a run, Huntsville started to make trouble after the first batter struck out. A single, a stolen base and a walk put the tying and winning runs on base. A passed ball put them in scoring position.

The next batter was a slight youngster, a Chicano named Navarro who'd put in a fine game in right field for the visitors. He took two pitches for balls and watched a strike cross his belt. Then the pitcher threw him a curve, and it had something on it—like maybe a dab of spit or Vaseline—because I could see the ball flutter weirdly. Navarro got a piece of it and sent a pop fly towering into foul territory down the left field line near the stands. Lonnie had taken off for it at the crack of the bat and raced after it with his back to home plate while the shortstop and left fielder converged on it as well. The left fielder called for it and waved his teammates off. By all rights, it belonged to him but Lonnie couldn't see or hear him because of the roar. Lonnie spied him at the last moment and hesitated. Unfortunately, the left fielder hesitated, too. The shortstop was too far away.

Lonnie dived and shot his glove out at ground level as the three fielders collided. Lonnie bounced off the left fielder's knees and rolled over waving his glove. Half in and half out of the webbing was the ball.

Many other players, even big-league pros, would have forgotten the situation in this triumphant moment. And, counting on that, the runner at third base alertly tagged up and sped for home. But Lonnie was heads-up all the way. From a sitting position, he whipped the ball to the catcher. It arrived simultaneously with the runner, who tried to dislodge it from the catcher's hands the same way Lonnie had done earlier. Only this time the catcher hung tough.

"Whaddya say? Whaddya say?" DePaw shouted hoarsely at me. "Major league material, hah, Mr. Bolt? All-star material?"

"Yeah," I said sadly. "All that. And an inmate of Bristow State Prison, too."

Chapter X

• • • •

The prison's visiting room was a large, long bullpen. It was brighter and cleaner than the rest of the joint, probably because it was the main point of contact with the outside world. It was painted robin's egg blue and its walls were decorated with sketches and paintings by inmates. Most of these were good and a few astonishingly good, gallery quality.

The room was divided lengthwise by a high partition of thick plate glass in which, at regular intervals, were embedded microphones and speakers. Every one of the twenty or twenty-five positions was occupied, and a bank of benches against the wall on my side was crowded with visitors anxiously awaiting their turn. There were easily identifiable types, dapper attorneys and distraught wives and mothers, and others more difficult to get a make on, furtive, suspicious-looking people with darting eyes, accomplices or accessories or something. Mostly they spoke in murmurs to the blue-clad men on the other side of the partition, but a few wept and wailed and pounded the glass with frustration. I felt my throat tightening and hoped desperately that they'd bring Lonnie out so I could flee this scene out of hell.

The guard by my side nudged me and jerked his head at a door through which Lonnie had just passed. Several cons noticed him and cheered and everything stopped while the rest of the inmates picked up the accolade, patting him on the buns or thumping his shoulder as he crossed to a door on the other side of the area. A guard admitted him and my own guard motioned me to a door on my own side corresponding to the one Lonnie had just entered. My guard lifted a heavy bolt and ushered me in.

The room was a dank stone-walled cube of stuffy air about twelve feet on a side with a high barred window through which a thin ray of sunlight sheared. Lonnie was standing with one foot upon a bench under that window, looking at me with curious expectation. The door slammed behind me with a huge metallic clunk and the guard, a portly man with a blotchy face and a blinking tic, folded his arms and leaned against the wall. I tried not to let his presence affect me but as Lonnie and I talked I began to feel as if I was broadcasting the dialogue to the rest of the prison over a loudspeaker.

Lonnie straightened as I crossed the room to shake his hand. He was even taller than I'd figured him for, maybe two inches over my own six-three. He wore faded denim jeans and a work shirt with his name and the number 58374 embroidered in navy thread on his breast pocket. His clothes appeared to be a size too small. The cuffs of his pants came above his ankles and his wrists stretched out of his shirt cuffs like a scarecrow's. My eyes flitted to those wrists, and I quickly understood whence the fantastic whippiness of his throw and his swing. They were like a bundle of BX cables with no discernible taper where they met his long, graceful hands. From time to time, my eyes would return to this remarkable portion of his anatomy. It seemed that every time he twiddled a finger the tendons in his wrist would ripple and quiver.

His face was a rugged block of many different planes. His complexion was pale, as might be expected of a con. His eyes were china blue, his hair a mop of wheat-colored locks longer than regulations permitted. I suspected the prison's officials were indulgent toward him because of his star status.

We shook hands. His grip was an iron sheath.

"Did they tell you. . .?" I asked.

"Yes, sir. You're Dave Bolt. Bonnie wrote me saying you might be paying me a visit. I'm really glad to see you, Mr. Bolt. But I'm not exactly sure how come you're here. Bonnie said you wanted to help me."

"I do, but I'm not sure how, myself."

He nodded with resignation, then shrugged. "D'ja see the game?"

"I sure did. There's a lot worse'n you playing big-league ball these days."

He smiled shyly. "Thank you. Coming from you, that means a lot to me."

"Yep. I daresay you could be the greatest ballplayer in prison history." He flinched at my irony but to underscore it I added, "Too bad nobody outside gives a shit."

He glowered. "Is this what you mean by helping me?"

"I'm sorry, son," I said, feeling a little guilty. "It's just that there's something about watching a kid like you pissing away all that talent. . ."

"Aw, what the hell, Mr. Bolt," he said airily. "Long as I get to play ball, it really doesn't matter where I do it."

"You couldn't possibly mean that." I searched his eyes. They were not the eyes of someone accustomed to concealing his feelings. Of course, he didn't mean it. But how else could he cope with his despair, save by sarcasm?

He sighed. "I just don't need anybody to tell me how fucked up my life is."

I looked uneasily over my shoulder at the guard, who was whistling silently, eyes roving the ceiling. "You were convicted of possession," I said in a low voice.

"Uh-huh."

"You claim you were framed."

"I know I was framed."

"But you won't tell who or why."

"My lawyer knows."

I raised my eyebrows. "But he won't say."

"Not without my permission, uh-uh."

"Who are you protecting?"

"Somebody."

"Can we home in a little sharper than that?"

He sighed heavily through clenched teeth. "Don't you think I would if I could? Jesus Christ, you think I'm doin' this 'cause I love stone walls and bars?"

We had a standoff, which was natural enough, seeing as how I'd offered him no inducement. But I'd thought about it on the drive up from Orange and prepared a tactic if my first assault netted me nothing. "Lonnie, you know I'm an agent. I represent ballplayers, professional ballplayers. Smitty Barnes is my client. Bates Lord, Rudolfo Blanco, Chuck Kluger—they're my clients, too."

"Yeah." He said it coolly, but I could tell he was impressed.

"I have a fair amount of influence," I said.

"I would guess."

"I'd like to see you play in the majors."

"It's too late for that, Mr. Bolt. Everyone that was interested in me dropped away after I got busted. Nobody'll look at me now. Even if I was paroled tomorrow, I'd be an untouchable. See, there's what's known as a stigma. . ."

"I know all about stigmas. But I'm not talking about a parole, Lonnie. I'm talking about, what if you were completely cleared? Pardoned. The conviction reversed."

"It can't ever happen, Mr. Bolt. Not without my spilling the whole story and I'm not about to do that." He looked down at his paint-stained shoes. When he looked up again there were tears in his eyes. "Fuckin' shit!" he sobbed, pounding his knee with his fist. His shoulders shook and he wept in long gusts punctuated by choked gurgles for a minute. I laid a hand on his shoulder. After a while, the outburst subsided and he caught his breath.

He sniffed and looked past me at the guard. "Hey, Winky, you got any of that bubblegum on you?"

The guard grinned and obligingly drew a handful of Bazooka out of his coat jacket. He came over and dropped them into Lonnie's big hand. "Sure, Lonnie. Anything for you."

"Winky, you're the best damn screw in this joint," Lonnie said, unwrapping a piece and stuffing it into his mouth.

"And you're my favorite fish, Lonnie-boy." Winky looked at me and squinched up his eyes. "If it was up to me, Mr. Bolt, I'd beat the answers out of this boy. Anything to spring him. He don't belong in this here shithole. They ain't a con or a bull in this whole damn prison wouldn't love to see Lonnie Raintree cut loose."

"I believe it," I said. Then I had a notion.

I pulled Winky aside and put my head close to his confidentially. "Winky, I think Lonnie wants to tell me something but he's a little uptight with you hanging around."

He twisted his lips. "Hell, Mr. Bolt, I can't leave you two alone. They'd have my ass. I mean, I know you're clean and all that, but just supposin' you slipped that boy a piece and he went and kilt hisself or his cellmate or one of the bulls or the Warden. It would be my ever-lovin' ass."

It was a convincing protest, but I didn't buy it.

I reached into my blazer and took out my wallet for the second time that day. "Tell me, old buddy, what's your favorite charity?"

He tilted his head reprovingly. "You don't take no for an answer."

"We're not talking about what I take, Winky. We're talking about what you take. What's your favorite charity?"

He blinked several times. "Well, now, I guess I'd have to say it's the Winky Walsh Foundation."

I grinned and pulled a pair of twenty-dollar bills out of my wallet.

"And then there's the Winky Walsh Trust, the Winky Walsh Retirement Fund, and the Winky Walsh Investment Syndicate."

I pulled out two more twenties, then a third. "And of course," I said, "leave us not forget the Winky Walsh Vacation Plan."

His hand hovered over the bills. "Vacation Plan? Can't hardly get to Nacogdoches on that. You know what the price of gas is up to today?"

I laid another twenty on him. He slid the wad of bills into his shirt pocket, unlocked the door, and looked at me, squinting through his twitching eyelids. "Just remember, it's my ass, Mr. Bolt."

"It's your ass, Winky."

He slipped outside and bolted the door.

Lonnie had been watching this episode with mouth wide open. "Gee, Mr. Bolt. . ."

"It'll come out of your salary one day," I said. "Now— how about we talk?"

He chewed vigorously on his Bazooka bubble gum, then took it out of his mouth, wrapped it in its original paper and put it in his shirt pocket for later. "You've met my girl, Bonnie, right?"

"Right."

"What'd you think of her?"

"Lovely kid, sweet kid."

"I wouldn't hurt her for the world."

I looked at him sharply, realizing he'd said something significant. "You mean, you'd go to prison first."

"Yes. Yes, exactly." He sat heavily on the bench, those fluid hands circumnavigating each other like a couple of otters making love. "A little over a year ago—New Year's Eve—there was this party?"

"In Brownsville?"

"Uh-huh. I didn't have a date, on account of Bonnie was in Amarillo visiting her aunt and uncle? So I went to this party stag, with four other guys, also ballplayers, friends of mine from high school days. Naturally, we all got a little, y'know, bombed?"

"On what? Grass?"

"Bourbon. I said bombed, not stoned. Mr. Bolt, may God strike me down if I've ever had one puff of marijuana."

"Toke," I corrected him. His unfamiliarity with the user's language was a point in support of his claim. "Go on."

"Well, there was this girl there, Billie-Ann Willitz? Sixteen years old and real pretty. I mean, she could of passed for twenty-one. I'd known her since she was a baby. She'd had a crush on me for the longest time but until that night, I always regarded her as a kid. But in the year or so since I'd seen her last—shee-it, you wouldn't believe how she'd bloomed." He emphasized this contention with cupped hands. "Now, I'd heard some stories about her."

"Like what?"

"Like, you know, she. . . uh. . . did it?"

"Did it, right."

"Well, she was a little high herself at this party, I'm not

sure on what and she started comin' on. Mostly with me. I was tempted, 'course, but I kept tellin' myself, shit, man, she's jail-bait. So she started coming on with the other guys and I got jealous. So. . ." He bit his lip, hoping I'd finish the sentence for him. I obliged him.

"So you took her upstairs and balled her."

"Wellll. . ." He shook his head with shame.

For a second I didn't understand. Then I snapped my fingers. "You mean, the other guys, too?"

"Uh-huh."

"All five of you?"

"Uh-huh."

"Nice. What happened then?"

"Nothing happened then."

Again I drew a blank for a moment or two. Lonnie was pounding his knee loudly. "Ah, you mean later," I said.

"Yup."

"She turned up in a family way," I groaned.

Lonnie rocked back and forth on his haunches, his face almost a prototype of shame.

I still didn't quite see the connection between this story and his imprisonment. "What happened then?"

"Well, she came to me and told me she'd, y'know, missed a couple months?"

"Yeah?" For a kid who'd had no compunctions about gang-shagging a teenager, he was amazingly delicate.

"She was really scared. So I asked her if she wanted to go to an abortionist? Well, she was even more scared of that. But I finally talked her into it—at least, so I thought. We were going to chip in, the five of us?"

"That was sporting of you."

He looked at me morosely. I couldn't make him feel any guiltier than he already felt. "I took her to this doctor we'd heard about in Delmita? But just as we're about to go in, she chickens out. Can't say as how I completely blame her. Outside of the doctor's office looked more tumbledown 'n Uncle Barney's henhouse. But it wasn't just she was scared, mind. She was also—well, her upbringin' was pretty strict. Southern Baptist."

I snorted, suppressing a laugh. Even Lonnie managed a slight smirk. "I guess that sounds strange, huh, Mr. Bolt? Considering how she'd got herself into this situation? Anyways, while we're driving back to Brownsville she says, 'Lonnie, I think the only right thing is for you to marry me.' Well shit, Mr. Bolt, I like to drove clear off the road. I stop the car and says, 'Me? Why me?' I mean hell, chances were only one out of five I'm the father. Plus, she'd been messing around with some other guys as well, so for all I know, it wasn't any of us five. But see, I was the only one she really liked."

"What did you do then?"

He gritted his teeth. "Well, I didn't do much of any-thing, to be truthful. I really didn't know what to do. I just told her again, she'd have to have an abortion. I mean, how could I of married her? I was going with Bonnie, don't you see?"

"Yes, I see. And Bonnie didn't know."

"God, no!"

"And she still doesn't."

"No."

The puzzle was beginning to take shape and I fingered the next piece. "So she went to her daddy?"

"Her daddy? Good Godamighty, no! It would of kilt him for certain. I told you, him and Mrs. Willitz is South-ern Baptists. No, she went to her brother Walt. Well, she didn't go to him, exactly. More like, he figured it out from the way she'd been behavin' and from. . . well, by that time, she was startin to get. . . y'know, visible?"

"Right."

"Now, Walt, he's a mean sumbitch. I mean, like mean."

He illustrated this by stretching his arm out and making claws with his fingers, like a menacing bear.

"Did she tell Walt how she'd gotten pregnant?"

"Only partially. See, she was too ashamed and too scared of her brother to tell him it had been. . . uh. . . y'know, more'n one guy."

"So she told him it was just you."

"Uh-huh. Well, the night she tells him, he comes after me and whips me pretty good. Not that I couldn't of took him if I'd been of a mind to. But when you don't feel you're in the right, you kinda lose your spunk, you feel you deserve a whippin', am I right? Anyways, he says to me, 'You're gonna marry my sister.' And I says, 'Walt, I just can't.'"

"Did you tell him about the other guys?"

"No. First of all, I wouldn't ever snitch on my buddies. And second of all, there was her reputation. I mean, even if Walt didn't beat her to death when he learnt the truth, she'd of still been ruined. I couldn't do that to her. I told Walt I was still ready to pay for an abortion but he wasn't about to hear of no abortion. See, Mr. Bolt, Brownsville ain't like New York City, where girls get knocked up as regular as prune juice, go to some clinic, and the next night they're ballin' their asses off again. Down there in Brownsville, gettin' pregnant out of wedlock is a sin."

That was true enough. I guess you get jaded living in the Big Apple and I'd come to take its chic cynical hedonism for granted. Listening to Lonnie's story was like blowing the dust off a shelf full of relics marked Honor, Justice, Propriety, Sobriety, Dignity, Chastity, and a dozen other virtues that smart New Yorkers just didn't have the time, money, or courage to afford. Though Lonnie's was a horror story, there was something comforting about the context of right and wrong out of which it was woven. It felt good to be back in a land where people still thought in such terms.

"What happened then, Lonnie?"

"Well, there wasn't nothin' for her to do but go to her folks and own up to what she'd done." He spoke the next sentence so softly it almost went by unheard. "Just about broke their hearts. Finally, they decided to send her away to have the baby. I went to Walt and offered to support her and the baby till she could find herself a husband."

"And he said. . .?"

"He said no thanks, he'd find another way to make me pay. I guess you can figure out how he done that."

"How did Walt get the dope he planted on your car?"

"In Brownsville, on the Meskin border?" he laughed.

"And you wouldn't defend yourself because. . ."

"Because Bonnie would find out."

"Where's Billie-Ann now?"

"Up in Goliad with some distant cousins or some-such. She had the baby—boy—and they made up some story about her bein' a widder. I guess she's gettin on all right." He stretched and looked up at the square of blue sky bisected by the bars of the window over our heads. "That's the story, Mr. Bolt. Maybe you can see a way out, but I can't."

"Oh, there's a way out," I said. "But it's going to cost you."

"I don't have any money."

"I wasn't talking about money," I said walking to the iron door and pounding on it.

Lonnie's high forehead was ridged. "I don't understand. You don't mean to say I'm gonna have to marry Billie-Ann?" He chased me across the room, distressed.

"You just think about it."

He cupped his cheeks in his big hands, then whipped me a threatening stare. "You're not going to tell Bonnie about all this, are you? I can't allow you to do that."

"No," I said, "I'm not going to tell her." The door swung open and Winky slipped inside as Lonnie opened his mouth to question my inflection of the sentence. "You'll be hearing from me, Lonnie," I said, exiting into the hot, stuffy, babble-filled visiting room. I couldn't get out of that joint fast enough.

Chapter XI

● ● ● ●

"Hello, Dave."

"Hello, Nancy."

She stood outlined by the half-open door, obviously glad to see me but as always, uncertain as to how to express it. A handshake was too skimpy, an embrace too ardent. There's never been an appropriate body language for ex-spouses who are still in love with each other. So she stood there, very pretty in a beige wool turtleneck dress, kind of paralyzed like a statue named "The Smile." I stood a little stiffly myself, waiting for her cue. Receiving none, I did what I felt like doing, which was to step up to her, put my hands on her cheeks, and hold a tender kiss on her lips.

"Come in," she said, gesturing at the unfamiliar apartment with an airy sweep of the hand. I was in a spacious foyer giving to a plant-filled living room furnished with a simplicity verging on austerity. Two low couches in tasteful floral print faced each other across a table that was nothing more than a slab of dark marble four inches off the floor. A single spotlight aimed at one wall and some dim bulbs beneath a display of modern prints and framed posters were the only illumination, giving the room a New York feel, though don't ask me to explain what I mean by that. Beyond the plants, a glass wall with sliding doors displayed the pulsing night skyline of Fort Worth. I shook my head with awe. It seemed as if every time I left that town, I came back to find a different contour on its skyline; this time, twin towers belonging to some insurance group, now straddling the freight yards beyond the Tarrant County Convention Center. Fort Worth, now part of something some promoters were calling the Southwest Metroplex (another term for the mishmash that had become Dallas, Fort Worth, and the stupendous airport in between), was so far from the Fort Worth I'd known as a kid, I couldn't honestly call it the same place.

"With all the money I send you, can't you afford more furniture?" I joked.

She launched a solemn defense of spareness in decorating, then caught herself mid-sentence. "You're teasing me."

I chucked her under the chin. "Of course. I like this place very much. Sure as hell is different from our old home on Trinity Road. In fact, I don't see a stick of furniture from there."

"I didn't. . . didn't want any of the old stuff."

"I understand. Ghosts and all that."

She dropped the subject like a hot rivet. "Your mom's been real nice to me. And business is picking up, too. Continental Airlines just asked me to redecorate their executive offices."

"Hey, nice going!"

I moseyed down a hallway and looked into a prim little bedroom wallpapered with photos and posters of rock stars. Nancy came up behind me and anticipated my questions. "Jody's at a girl friend's house, pajama party. I didn't tell her you were in town. I thought tomorrow you might like to take her to—"

"I've got to move on early tomorrow morning," I said, gulping guiltily.

She nodded with resignation. She'd expected it, but she never did get entirely used to my flying visits. "I'll call her and ask her to come home tonight, then." She went to the phone ensconced in a niche in the foyer wall.

"Not quite yet. Let's just talk a while."

She set the phone back on its cradle. "Oh, I forgot to tell you." She pulled a sheet of memo paper off the pad beside the phone. "A Dennis Whittie called. Said he'd call you back. He didn't leave a message or a number or anything."

"Thanks."

"I didn't have a chance to pick up a cake, but we do have some chocolate chip cookies and Oreos in the pantry. I know how much you like them. I'll put up some coffee."

I smiled to myself. Nancy never offered me alcoholic beverages, ever. And who could blame her, considering what alcoholic beverages had done to our marriage? Even when I swore up and down I'd licked the problem and could imbibe with moderation, she never trusted me. "Cookies and coffee'll be fine," I said, trailing her into a gay, canary yellow kitchen whose walls were covered with pretty watercolors of fruits and vegetables.

Her motions around the kitchen were brisk and businesslike, almost exaggeratedly so. She was tall, blond, and leggy, in the best tradition of athletes' wives—ex-wives, pardon me. (As my divorce consisted of somebody slapping a paper in my hand while I groveled under a barstool, I could never quite accept it as a reality.) I noted some lines of maturity on her face but they only enhanced it with the allure of experience. About three extra pounds evenly distributed over her torso did no harm, either. She was perhaps more attractive than I'd ever seen her. I wanted to make love to her—we always slept together when I visited—but she moved with a kind of hostessy ceremony that forbade intimacy. It made me feel like a guest and I wondered if she was aware of the effect, and indeed, whether she'd deliberately produced it.

"Have you seen your mom?" she asked.

"I just came from there."

"She looks well, doesn't she?"

"Never changes, thank God." It had been wonderful seeing that proud ramrod of a matriarch, if only for an hour, and I'd come away feeling gladder than ever to find another island of constancy in a protean world. I looked at Nancy hard, studying her, wondering why she was laying on all this cordiality and small talk. One answer occurred to me. "Have you been, uh, seeing anybody?"

"No, not really. Been too busy. I'm really into my decorating career now."

"But you're not decorating now," I said.

"Hm?"

"I mean, you've been entertaining me as if I was a client or something."

She opened her mouth to protest but knew it wouldn't hold water. "I guess I have been."

I clutched her hand. "What is it, Nancy? You got more defenses than the Miami Dolphins."

She pulled her hand back and returned to her busywork, laying cookies on a plate and filling a little pitcher with cream. "Look, Dave, I don't know how to say this, but. . . I think we should face up to the fact that things just aren't the same anymore. When I moved here from Trinity Road, I left an awful lot of crap behind me, and I'm not referring to furniture from our marriage. I've realized. . . well, it's sunk in that we're not married and never will be again. I've got to make my own way, start a new life for myself. I've lived for years dreaming that we'd be reconciled but now I see that for what it is—just a dream."

She paused to take the perking coffee off the stove and pour out two cups. Even as she did, even as I intuited what was coming down, I couldn't help but admire her beautifully muscled arms and the enticing way her hair fell over her cheeks as she fussed with the cookie plate.

"Now, these visits of yours," she continued, setting my snack in front of me. "Oh, I love seeing you, don't get me wrong. And the. . . and the sex is—well, it's certainly not the sex. I mean, it's not the performance," she stammered, looking terribly uncomfortable in her effort to be precise. "But you see, each. . . each session leaves me lonelier than the last. And now that I'm in a new apartment with a new career and new opportunities to. . . to meet people, I can't afford that anymore." "That" was defined by an index finger pointing to her bedroom. "I've got to streamline my life, don't you see? And for us to continue our involvement . . . at least, in the sense of. . . oh shit, Dave, help me out. You know what I mean!" She slopped coffee over the rim of her cup. Her hands were trembling almost violently.

"You mean you don't want to sleep with me anymore," I said. I stated it matter-of-factly, concealing how much it hurt me. But what sense was there in making a hard decision harder by making her feel guilty about it?

She sniffed and wiped her nose delicately with the back of her hand. "It's funny," she said, clearing a rasp out of her throat. "I pictured this conversation a hundred times in my mind and it was always so easy. But now that you're here, I look at you and ask myself, 'What are you doing, Nancy?' I feel so natural with you, it's like nothing ever happened."

"But something has happened."

"If you mean someone else, please believe it has nothing. . ."

"No, I mean, something inside you."

"Yes. Yes, that's very true. But I wasn't sure you'd understand that."

"Oh, I understand it real well."

"But you're hurt. You're angry, I can see."

"No, I'm not. Well, yes, I reckon maybe a little. But not because my vanity's been injured. It has nothing to do with that."

She gazed at me attentively, waiting for me to frame it into words. I sought them, found them, assembled them as best I could. "I guess I'm just seeking a few things in this world I can trust to sit still for ten minutes at a time. My life has become so goddam busy and complicated. I turn my back for a day and nothing's the same when I turn back around. Christ, look at Fort Worth! I'd hoped, you see, that you, at least. . . well, I can't even count on you. And. . . shoot, I'm almost afraid to see what's become of Jody!"

"She's shooting up like a mushroom, Dave."

"That's just what I don't want to hear. I just want my little baby the way she's always—"

Where the tears came from, I don't know but they'd rushed into and out of my eyes almost before I realized the feeling was there. Nancy's arms were around me and the softness of her breasts comforted my warm cheek. The outburst, or maybe call it breakdown, lasted only a few moments.

I finally caught my breath and pushed Nancy away, sipped some coffee and sat limply at the table, wondering where this freight train of feeling had come from. Nancy stood over me, wringing her hands and biting her lip. That's when the phone rang.

Nancy caressed my arm as she pushed past me to answer it. I got up and went to the kitchen sink, splashed some water on my face, and dried off with a paper towel.

Nancy looked in. "It's for you. It's that Dennis Whittie again."

"Thanks." I avoided her look as I crossed the foyer. I picked up the phone. "Hello, Dennis?"

"Dave? You all right?"

"Sure, why?"

"You sound like you got a cold."

"No, I've just been crying," I said.

"Sure you have. The last time you cried was when you bet on Baltimore in Super Bowl III."

"What's up?"

"Good news, bad news. Which do you want first?"

"Bad."

"The bad is that Pinky Ryan doesn't know where his daughter is and I think I believe him."

"Why do you believe him?"

"Because the Dennis Whittie Patented Testicle Twist is guaranteed to elicit the truth, the whole truth, and nothing but the truth, or God help you."

"Jesus, Dennis."

"You did say anything goes."

"Yes, but. . ."

"Can I tell you something, Dave? If they had let me use the Dennis Whittie Patented Testicle Twist on Erlichman, Haldeman, Mitchell, and Dean, I'd have saved the taxpayer millions of dollars in court costs."

I laughed and the laughter was a tonic. "All right, what's the good news?"

"The good news is that your hunch about Mark Fioretta was right."

"Aha. I finally did something right."

"Sounds that way. You told me that Ryan and Fioretta

left the United Steelworkers to start their own union, right? Then the two of them fought and Ryan squeezed his partner out, and Fioretta started this rump union of his own, the UCB? Well, these two chaps are intensely jealous of each other and have been picking each other off for years. Now, for sixty-four thousand dollars and a chance to beat the other couple, do you happen to remember why Ryan and Fioretta broke with each other?"

"Umm. . ."

"It was over the issue of violence, baby, violence. Fioretta liked to throw his muscle around, but Ryan would have none of it. Okay, now we get down to the nitties and the gritties. Were you aware that Fioretta, early this year when he heard that Pinky Ryan was wooing the Players Association, made a pitch for them, too?"

"That's right. The commissioner did tell me, the day I had lunch with him, but I'd forgotten. But Fioretta was never in serious contention, was he?"

"No, not after an investigation of his union disclosed a history of strong-arm tactics, including arson, burglary, vandalism, suspected homicide, and hitting below the belt. Plus alleged tie-ins with those happy, carefree, artless people back in Sicily."

"So my theory was correct, Pinky Ryan thinks Fioretta had Willie mauled out of jealousy?"

"Jealousy? Oh, it goes a lot deeper than jealousy, cousin. Fioretta realized that if Ryan's courtship of the Players Association was successful, Ryan's union would become a major labor force in this country, eclipsing Fioretta's UCB and eventually, perhaps, destroying it entirely. So when Fioretta heard a rumor—or maybe a spy told him—that Ryan and the Players Association were actually going to make a deal, Fioretta had to do something to discredit his rival."

"So when Willie Hesketh announced he was driving down to Florida—"

"Fioretta saw his opportunity, exactly. He knew suspicion for the beating would fall on Ryan and make him look like a gangster. The Players Association would pull out of its agreement with Ryan and the strike would break."

"Which is exactly what happened."

"Yo. But caveat, Dave—this is still only a theory and Pinky Ryan's theory, at that."

"True. But it's as good as any I've heard. Better, actually, because it makes more sense. But you're right, it's still only a theory. What about Fiona? What did Ryan say about Fiona?"

"She's off somewhere looking for the goon who lost an eye. If she can find him and link him to Fioretta, we've made our case."

"But Ryan doesn't know where she is."

"Nope. She was afraid he'd worry so she didn't even tell him."

I pounded the wall with my fist. "Why are they so goddam secretive about this?"

"It's their personal vendetta, and they don't want any outsiders horning in on their action. They've reserved the pleasure of vengeance for themselves."

"Stupid, stubborn. . ."

"What do I do now, Dave?"

"You move in with Ryan, is what you do, and cling to him till Fiona phones in. The second she does, call me."

"Where you gonna be?"

"I was planning to go to the Honchos' spring training camp in Lubbock tomorrow, to speak to Ruby Swanson, who's the last concrete suspect on my list. If I draw a blank with Swanson, and haven't heard from you, I'll fly back to New York tomorrow afternoon, take care of business, and wait for you to call." I gave him the Lubbock number where he could reach me and instructed him to call Trish and turn over to her whatever agency negotiations he was in the midst of. "Oh, yes," I remembered, "call the commissioner and tell him everything we've just discussed except that I wagered on the Super Bowl. Tell him I think we ought to have Mark Fioretta watched."

"Check."

I hung up the phone and stood dumbly for a minute, reeling with the weight of Dennis's input and the conflicting emotions it had precipitated. My relief at the prospect of breaking the logjam of false leads in this damn Hesketh case was balanced by worry about Fiona. She'd taken upon herself her father's part in the feud with the man who—if my theory was correct—had destroyed her father's dream. But God only knew what kind of trouble her damned Irish pigheadedness was going to get her into. Surely, she couldn't be so all-fired naive as to think she could walk into a pack of cutthroats and say, "Ringolevio, one-two-three, citizen's arrest!" and expect them to come docilely away with her.

My sense of helplessness at that moment was all but paralyzing. I wanted to act, somehow. But how? What could I do, really, but wait for that call from Dennis, if it ever came?

I shook the bogeys out of my head and started back to the kitchen.

The sight of Nancy standing statuesquely in the doorway of the bedroom brought me up short.

She'd changed out of her dress into a sheer powder blue chiffon, full-length nightgown, so transparent in the soft backlight from the night table that I could trace perfectly the silhouette of her parted legs and see the cherry color of her erect nipples jutting through the wispy fabric. I knew that gown so well. She'd worn it on our wedding night and brought it out over the years for particularly seductive occasions. Her eyes were sloe and sleepy, her lips shiny and moist. She breathed slow and deep, stretching the gown over her breasts in rhythmic pulses.

"Nancy Bolt, what the hell are you doing?"

She extended a long white arm and beckoned to me with a subtle toss of her head. "Come."

I took two steps into the hallway and stopped. "I don't understand. What was that whole song-and-dance you gave me in the kitchen?"

She shrugged, a childlike gesture that only augmented her intense womanhood. And she smiled ingenuously. "The spirit was willing but my flesh is weak. Come," she said again, twiddling her index finger.

If Nancy's flesh was weak, there's no word to describe the feebleness of my own as I gazed at the figure poised expectantly only a foot or two away, luring me to her bed with that lovely outstretched arm. Yet I hung back and to this day I'm not sure I understand what kept me from reaching out to complete the circuit, taking her in my arms and bearing her off to bed. I like to think I did it out of love and respect for her but knowing myself, that sounds a little too noble. More likely, at that moment I was gripped by a kind of elevated romantic foolishness my ancestors called chivalry. I hated them for having passed it on to me through their genes because the less gallant side of me wished nothing more than to take advantage of poor Nancy's weak flesh. But there's no speaking for genes. "Nancy, have you considered. . .?"

"While you were on the phone I did some thinking, Dave. Yes, it's true I'm trying to start a new life here and all that. But I also realized, you can't cut everything behind you completely. Some things you carry with you no matter where you go. Some you carry to the grave, I suppose."

"And what have you carried with you from Trinity Road?"

She didn't hesitate. "The way I feel about you. I brought along my love for you."

I leaned heavily against the hall closet door and sighed. "Uh-uh. You brought your weak flesh with you. That's not the same thing." She arched her eyebrows and looked at me seriously. "You told me you hate yourself more and more every time we sleep together. How do you think you're going to feel tomorrow morning after breaking a solemn vow you made to yourself?"

Her breasts rose and fell heavily. I didn't think I was getting through to her.

"Let me tell you something, Nancy," I said quietly. "I've been an addict myself, after a fashion—and you know which fashion. I know what it's like to swear off a bad habit in the morning and give in to temptation an hour later. You can loathe yourself so awful you want to die. I can't let you do this to yourself."

I was right. I wasn't getting through to her. She stepped forward, closing the gap of resistance like an electric spark jumping across damp air. She threw herself into my arms and clung to me with incredible feline ferocity. "I don't care, Dave. I just want you, now. I'm so lonesome here, honey, so scared. . ."

She was trembling and panting and thrust her breasts against my chest and ground her crotch against mine maddeningly. I put my hands on her shoulders and pushed her away. "That's not good enough, Nancy. Lookee, what you said to me in the kitchen—sure, it hurt me. But I knew it was right. You were speaking with your heart then, not with your. . . with your pussy like you are now. I was hurt, sure, but I decided I got to accept it. I accept it so completely I can't let you go back on it, even though I'd like to carry you into that bedroom and screw your eyes out."

She rushed me again, almost hysterical, clawing my chest. "Please, Dave, just this last time. I'll be strong from then on, I know it."

"Darling, I just can't."

"Dave, lay me, please, please!" she sobbed, falling to her knees and pressing kisses against my fly. She fumbled with the zipper and reached inside. Her hands were as cool and sensitive and knowing as they'd ever been as they found my flesh and manipulated it. This was hitting a man below the belt. My resolution was draining as if punctured by a dum-dum bullet. In another second my reserve of that virtue, such as it was, would be exhausted. I had to do something.

I took a handful of her golden hair and yanked her head away. She sprawled on the carpet and I walked away. Or maybe hobbled is a better description of my mode of locomotion—she'd damn near bent me in half with desire.

I went into the kitchen, found her cigarettes, and lit one with trembling hands. I smoked it frenetically, listening to her terrible sobs. After a few minutes, they subsided. I heard the rustling of her gown as she picked herself up and got herself together.

Then I heard her pick up the phone and dial a number. Her voice, nasal and hoarse from crying, drifted into the kitchen. "Hello, may I speak to Jody?" There was a moment's pause. Then: "Hello, duckling. Guess what? Your daddy's here! Yes, right now. Can you come home right away?"

Chapter XII

• • • •

I sat in the half-empty bleachers waiting for Ruby Swanson. Lubbock's midday sun was surprisingly hot for March but then I realized the ballpark walls were probably checking the norther that had nipped me when I got out of the taxi. I looked at my watch, then back at the game just in time to see one of those sparkling plays that make you exult in the simple things of life, like a good ball game on a warm day.

The Omaha Honchos were hosting the Oakland A's for this exhibition game. The A's were ahead 7-6 in the sixth inning but the Honchos had men on first and second with one out and were threatening. With Honcho right fielder Mickey Rankin batting, the count one-and-one, manager Bill Sarni called for a hit-and-run play. Rankin, a powerful lefty, timed a Vida Blue fast ball perfectly and hit a whistler down the first base line, a real grass-cutter that short-hopped in front of Gene Tenace at first, whirled out of his glove, and spun between his legs just behind him. It lay in that blind spot just behind your butt so that no matter which way you turn, it's just out of your line of vision. Tenace looked this way and that, bewildered while half his bench pointed at the ball. But Dick Green, the brilliant second baseman who'd darted automatically to his left at the crack of the bat, came up behind Tenace, dived between his legs, grabbed the ball with his bare hand while on his stomach, then stretched out with his empty glove to tag first base—which is perfectly legal. Green's tag beat Rankin by half a step.

Meanwhile, Manny Cirillo, who'd reached third on the hit-and-run, was signaled by his third base coach to try for home and the tying run. It was a good call, seeing as how Dick Green was sprawled flat on his stomach, incapable of throwing in that position. But what the coach didn't figure on was Gene Tenace. Tenace ripped the ball out of Green's bare hand and rifled it to catcher Ray Fosse a step ahead of the sliding runner for the third out.

An exuberant whoop came unbidden to my throat. It wasn't just for the play—hell, you almost come to take brilliance for granted when you watch the A's—but for the whole wonderful goddam institution of baseball. This hardy organism had somehow managed to weather the attempts of players, owners, the press, the TV boys, the union organizers, the gamblers and petty hustlers, and just about everyone else to destroy it. When all was said and done it was still, as I'd said to Fiona that day at lunch, fun. Baseball was going to be all right. Baseball was going to survive. Baseball was alive and well and entertaining in Lubbock, Texas.

I was even overjoyed to see the Honchos boot the ball all over the infield in their half of the inning, giving Oakland two insurance runs. Errors were part of the fun of baseball, too, though the Honchos were so maladroit they'd become the laughingstock of the major leagues.

"Can you believe that, fachrissakes? Can you fucking-A believe that?" It was the gravelly voice of Ruby Swanson, the Honchos' owner. I felt a heavy hand on my shoulder as he negotiated the unstable planks of the bleachers. "You'd think they'd be better than last year, wouldn't you? They're worse! Worse! You know what?" he grunted as he lowered himself onto the plank beside me. "I might as well withdraw my money from the bank and throw it out of my airplane."

The plank jounced me as his butt landed on it. I looked at the heavy, flabby man dressed flamboyantly in matching canary golfing slacks, polo shirt, and peaked cap. His belly hung obscenely over the belt of his trousers like sausage stuffing emerging from a grinder.

Ruby Swanson was the kind of man I don't like under any circumstances, but least of all as the owner of a professional team. I wish the criteria for owning a team were as stringent as they are for playing on one. Depressingly, money is pretty much the only one. Swanson had made his in trucking and had put together a syndicate of petit bourgeoisie—what my daddy called "po' millionaires"—to pick up the ailing Padres when they shifted out of San Diego.

He was one of the new breed of owners who see possession of a ball club as an ego trip and a tax shelter and who are incapable of leaving the running of the game to the professionals. He was a loudmouth and a glad hander and you could drive his fleet of trucks through the gaps in his understanding of baseball or baseball players. But he'd paid his dues and that meant I owed him the same homage I owed a Horace Stoneham or a Phil Wrigley. It galled me and I had to hobble my temptation to dump on the man.

"Well, now, Bolt, what brings you here? Does Joe Michaels want to get out of his contract?" Michaels, the Honchos' left fielder, was my client.

"No, it's nothing like that, Mr. Swanson. I'm here on another kind of business entirely."

"I hope you got an infielder for me. I swear to Christ, I'll kiss your ass right here and now if you've got an infielder for me. I mean, one with only one thumb on each hand."

I smiled. "No, it's about Willie Hesketh."

He looked at me blankly. His eyes were washed-out hazel embedded in fat. I could detect no response, though after last night's conversation with Dennis I'd been pretty sure this was going to be a wasted trip.

Swanson made a clucking sound. "Helluva shame, about Hesketh. He was your client, if I remember rightly."

"Yes."

"Helluva shame. Well, anyway, what's it got to do with me?"

"I thought you might have some theories about who caused his 'accident'." I delivered the statement neutrally and devoid of suggestiveness.

"Theories? Everybody knows who did it."

"They do?"

"Sure. Buddy Gilpin and his Commie friends. I can't believe they haven't been arrested already, fuckin' Commie bastids. They ought to be hung. At least they ought to be banned from baseball. That guy comes up to bat, my pitchers will have instructions to chuck at his skull."

"It hasn't been proved, Mr. Swanson. Nothing's been proved, about Gilpin or anybody else. That's why I'm still looking for some answers."

He folded his arms and looked at me with a hint of suspicion for the first time. "So let me ask you again. What brings you here?"

"I wanted to ask you about a certain remark you made to Sam Metcalf a short time before the incident."

He searched the sky for the memory but there was no recognition in his eyes when he looked back at me. "I made a lot of remarks to Sam Metcalf. Which one do you mean?"

"You said you would break the strike 'by whatever means are necessary,' at least according to Sam."

He leaned away from me, looking shocked and dismayed. "Now whoa, whoa, hold your horses! A man says a lot of things when his nuts are in a vise."

"I know. I want to know if you meant that particular one, that's all."

He took off his cap and mopped his head with the back of a hairy wrist. "Bolt, you've got to understand something about me. I'm a highly excitable person. I laugh easily and I get sore easily, do you see what I'm getting at? I could blow my top one minute, an hour later I don't even remember what it was all about. Now, take that strike."

"Yes, let's take that strike."

"All right. My nerves were frayed ragged. First the players make demands so outrageous, there's no possible way to meet them without the owners going completely bankrupt. That's bad enough, but then the owners start talking about shutting down the season. Now look, I have some money, but I don't have money to carry a baseball team for a year. I can't even write that off, and believe me, I write off everything but my wife's diaphragm. So there I was, sitting with an investment of millions, a responsibility to my partners in the syndicate, to the fans and the ballplayers and my friends at the bank, and I'm watching it spin around the toilet like a big pile of shit. Don't tell me you wouldn't say a few things of an irate nature to Sam Metcalf!"

"I might. But I'd still like to know what you had in mind, exactly, when you made that remark to him. I mean, what did you contemplate doing? What would you have done if the Willie Hesketh incident hadn't broken the strike?"

He held his sweating palms up to the sky. "Who the hell knows? I really don't know. But you got to understand one thing, Bolt, the happiest moment of my life came when your client announced he was going to walk through that picket line. Because that's when I said to myself, it's all over, kids, that's the beginning of the end. Once you rupture the unity of the strikers, even if it's only one scab who gets away with it, that strike is as good as broken. Take my word for it, Bolt. I know all about strikes. Don't forget, I went to school in the trucking industry."

"I know. I'm trying to find out what you learned there."

He looked at me sharply, reminding me of a wild boar contemplating a charge. "Bolt, I think I care for you very little."

I shrank back a little, sensing I'd pushed the man almost to the wall. But the question I'd traveled the length and breadth of Texas to ask remained unanswered, and I wasn't going to let his bluster deter me from asking it. "Let's face it, Mr. Swanson, everyone knows the trucking industry is controlled—"

I got only as far as this preface before the boar charged and for a pudgy man, he was quick and strong. He grabbed me by the shirt and yanked me clear into his lap, holding me an inch away from his face. His respiration was stertorous and his breath rank. I stayed loose, sensing he'd go no further.

His hands trembled and his eyes blazed. When he finally released me, it was with a shove that almost toppled me out of the bleachers. "Sonnyboy, I'd like you to leave the premises and I don't want to see your face again till it's accompanied by an apology. Meanwhile, you think about why I or any other owner would want Willie Hesketh beaten up when he represented the key to our victory over the players. Hah? You make sense out of that, I'll give you these wrists, you can put handcuffs on them and take me to jail. Until then, if it gets back to me you've been talking like this about me to anybody else, I'm going to take you to court for slander and suck your assets so dry you'll make a Bowery derelict look like a prince. Now, get the fuck out of here."

I got the fuck out of there, not because I was afraid of Swanson, but because I was simply convinced he was right. Or let's say, I was predisposed to believe him in light of Dennis's call from Pittsburgh the night before. In fact, had I known last night where Fiona was, I wouldn't have bothered to go to Lubbock at all.

I found a phone booth outside the stadium and called the Holiday Inn in Lubbock where the Honchos stayed during spring training. I'd given that number to Dennis and hoped with all my heart there'd be a message for me from him about Fiona. But there was none. Might as well return to New York. I looked at my watch. The next flight out of Dallas to New York left in two hours. I could make the connection from Lubbock with time to spare and I had an idea about what to do with that extra time.

I walked back into the stadium.

I found Ruby Swanson in front of the Honcho dugout talking to his manager, Bill Sarni, the former great St. Louis Cardinal catcher. Clinging to Swanson's arm was a lissome blonde whom he undoubtedly introduced as his niece. I stood near the right field foul line waiting to catch Swanson's attention. I finally got it and for the first time understood the true meaning of "jaundiced eye". It, along with the face that went with it, turned positively bile green at the sight of me. He detached himself from his cupcake and waddled up to me, thrusting his belly arrogantly against mine. "What'd I just tell you, smartass?"

"You said you wanted an apology. I brought you one, plus something else."

"Make it fast and make it good. That young lady is supposed to blow me in half an hour."

"I've got an infielder for you."

"That's even better than an apology. Who is he?"

"I'd rather not mention his name just yet. But he's great and you can have him cheap." I didn't add he could have him if and when the kid got out of prison.

"Compared to my infielders, anybody who can field a stationary baseball is great. Can you get him up here for a tryout?"

"It'll take a week or two."

"The season begins in a week or two."

"This guy's worth waiting for."

"What are you asking for him?"

"The minimum starting salary, no bonus, and a lift to the airport."

"You got it," he wheezed.

"What about her?" I said, gesturing at his girlfriend.

"You want her, I'll throw her into the bargain."

"No, I meant what are you going to do about her while you're driving me to the airport?"

Swanson put his arm around me and started for the exit.

"Bolt, I can always get a blow job but I can't always get a good infielder."

Chapter XIII

• • • •

It was early evening when my taxi pulled up in front of the Lincoln Building. New York City was just catching its second breath; Work City had faded out; Fun City was fading in. The air was chill, at least to one coming off a tour of the Southwest but there was also an ineffable promise of spring wafting through the canyon between my office building and Grand Central Terminal.

I had to sign in with the guard at the lobby entrance and I was the only passenger in the elevator normally jammed with humanity on its way to conducting urgent business during the day. I got off at the eighteenth floor and walked to my office, my heels tattooing noisily on the marble floor of the corridor. The echoing racket was joined by the tap-tap of a lonely typewriter inside Suite 1810-1812.

I inserted my key in the door and stepped inside. The lights were ablaze, Trish's way of making herself feel secure when she was alone in the office. I jiggled the doorknob noisily and slammed the door so as not to sneak up and scare her witless. She sat in her office, profile to me, hammering out what looked like a contract, her tongue flicking between her lips in a gesture of concentration that had always endeared me to her when it wasn't downright arousing me. She had a tweed jacket on over a voluminous silk blouse and it made her look almost overweight. One look at the tight, smooth skin of her face told you the bulky appearance of her body was an illusion.

"I hope you're not an intruder," she said without looking up from her typewriter, "because I have some very strong opinions on the subject of rape."

"No, just me."

"Gimme one more minute," she said,

"Take your time. I want to check out the log." I entered my own office and sat down at my desk and started to study the daily activity record I'd asked Trish and Dennis to keep for me whenever I went out of town. It was all there in apple pie order, phone messages, summaries of important letters, transactions, status of negotiations, daily receipts, and even gossip, an item I'd specially requested for inclusion in the log. Rumors in the sports business are as vital as they are in the entertainment business even though half of them turn out to be false. And besides, there are few things I love more than good, vicious gossip.

The typing in the next room stopped and Trish staggered into my office, yawning. She stretched, pulling her body taut. Not long ago, dressed as she once did in the skimpiest of fashions, I'd have had to avert my eyes to keep from being lured to my doom by her svelte beauty. Now she was just a tired executive trying to shake off fatigue. And yet. . .

I gazed at her and saw something I'd never seen before. "May I say something bold?"

She blinked. "Huh?"

"I find you more attractive tonight than I can ever remember."

She brushed some hair out of her eyes. "You've got to be crazy. I'm wearing a suit thicker than medieval armor, my nose is glossier than the skating rink in Rockefeller Center, my eyes must look like two cherries in a bowl of buttermilk, and my hair is Yech City."

"I know."

"I think we both need a drink." She went to my bar and mixed me my traditional; she took Scotch and water.

"I know what it is," I resumed speaking on the wings of an impulse whose origins mystified me. "It's that I've never seen you unconscious of your beauty. I mean, you're so wrapped up in your work, you haven't got time to flaunt yourself the way you used to."

"I'm getting old."

"You're getting. . . very lovely."

She put her hands on her hips and tilted her head. "Dave, why are you coming on like this?"

"Jesus," I said, scratching my head, "I don't know myself. I just feel like. . ." I put my drink down, got up and went around to her side of the desk. I put my arms around her waist and drew her to me. She relented, letting the contours of her body coalesce with mine. She closed her eyes and her lips went soft as I kissed her. For a moment she was all yielding and I felt myself swept by an urge of cyclonic magnitude. I ran my hands under her blouse and pressed my lips to the warm flesh of her graceful neck.

Suddenly her hands were against my chest, prying me away.

Panting, she walked to my couch and dropped down heavily. "I cannot fucking believe this," she muttered, as much to herself as to me. I stood awkwardly, trying to make sense of it myself. "For three years I do everything but lash you to a bed to get you to make love to me, and now, when I've given up on you, when I'm exhausted and preoccupied with my work and I look like death warmed over and have my period of all times, you lunkhead, now you want to go to bed with me. I could absolutely kill you."

I advanced a step and said, "It's never too late."

She held me off with upraised hands. "But it is, for fun and games, anyway."

"Uh-oh. Are you gonna go into this marriage number again?"

"Yeah, anything wrong with that?" She was panting harder than ever but from anger, not arousal.

"Yes, it's out of character."

"I think you're a little out of touch with my character or haven't you noticed I'm not the free spirit I was when you hired me?"

"Come on, Trish. A few responsibilities don't make a girl a spinster."

"I happen to have turned twenty-five two days ago, and thanks, incidentally, for forgetting my birthday."

I laughed. "So? Now that you're twenty-five, you've automatically got to get married?"

"No, but I can't be as casual about my relationships as I used to be."

"We never had a casual relationship," I said, chuckling harder. "I'm proposing we make up for lost time."

"Dave, I think you've been under a strain lately. You're not thinking. Go home and take a cold shower and get a good night's sleep. Tomorrow you'll wake up and be the same big prick I've adored from afar for all these many years."

I leaned heavily on the edge of my desk. "I suppose you're right. I don't know what got into me."

"I know what didn't get into me," she sighed, downing the rest of her drink. "Besides, Roy Lescade will be here any minute."

"Roy? What the hell for?"

"He's been bugging me hourly about when you're due back, so I told him you were coming in this evening and he said if you didn't see him this very evening you'd better look under the hood of your car before you start the engine."

"Aw, balls! I was really hoping to duck him."

"Unless I mistake that shuffling noise coming down the hall, there's no way of doing that."

"Double balls," I muttered, stealing one last glance at Trish as I realized that, sexually speaking, I'd been at both ends of the same shotgun within the last twenty-four hours, first Nancy, then her.

I had no more time for such ruminations, as I had to compose myself for Roy Lescade's grilling. A moment later the door opened and my dear old friend ambled in, looking, as usual, like a hamper of soiled laundry. He studied us both and must have picked up certain vibrations. "Looks like I'm breaking up a party," he said, going straight to my bar and fishing the branch water out of the secret cache where I hide it from non–Good Old Boys. He helped himself to a splash and a healthy six fingers of bourbon.

"I didn't know you were Roving Correspondent for Screw," I said.

"Roy's just jealous because he has designs on me," Trish said smiling.

"Then at least come up to my place and let me show you my designs," he countered.

"Thanks, I'll take a rain check," she said. "In fact, make that a Doomsday check." She put her jacket on and made to leave.

"Aw, stick around so's I have something pretty to look at," Roy urged.

"Yes, do," I said. "I want you to be in on this conversation. There's something I want you to do."

She shrugged and sat down.

Roy swizzled his drink and said, "Well, now, what have we learned from our tour of the glorious Southwest?"

"I've learned that one week without your face is like three weeks' vacation in Bimini. I've also learned that there's a helluva lot of smoke billowing around the Willie Hesketh incident, but so far I haven't been able to raise any fire."

"Then let's talk about the smoke."

"Uh-uh. You know what they say about speculation on the Kung Fu program."

"What's that?"

"'He who speculates on beating-up of ballplayers is like unto one who sniffeth the pink sunset on wings of song.'"

Roy glared at me. "Now I have one for you. 'He who trieth to jerketh off ace reporter gets toe of boot up asseth.'"

"I'm sorry, Roy. You got to give me a few more days. I promised you the exclusive, and that promise still holds. But I still have things to work out." He opened his mouth to protest, but I switched subjects instantly. "Meanwhile, I have a progress report on Lonnie Raintree."

"Lonnie Raintree is small potatoes. I didn't come here for that."

"It's the best I can do for you now."

He emitted a long bovine sigh.

"I visited him in prison and got him to 'fess up," I explained. "It seems that the guy who planted that dope in Lonnie's car was getting even with him for knocking up his sister and refusing to marry her."

Roy reluctantly dragged his attention to the matter. "Which is why he couldn't tell Bonnie and chose to take the rap."

"Well, that's most of it. The rest of it is that Lonnie's not sure he's the father. He was only part of what this gal, I know in publishing, calls a multiple submission."

"You mean a gang-bang."

"Uh-huh. But the sister, the knock-upee, told her brother that Lonnie was the only one, so he's it."

"I see. What happens now?"

"Well, between a dose of life in stir and some cogent reasoning on my part, I think he's ready to come around."

"To marrying the girl?"

"Uh-huh. I told him if he agreed to do that, I could have him out of prison practically overnight. What's more, I could have him in another uniform the next day—Ruby Swanson of the Honchos is ready to deal for him."

"What do you want from me?"

"You said you thought you could prevail on the judge who tried Lonnie and on the governor to push all the legal details through—chop-chop."

"Yes, I can do that," he said, grunting. I could read his thoughts. He'd come here to get a story and ended up with a boring assignment from which he could derive no benefit, except maybe a minor article.

Trish looked at me expectantly. "You said there was something you wanted me to do?"

"Yes. I want you to call Commissioner Bailey and ask him what his position is on having an ex-convict play in the major leagues. Tell him everything I've told you and do what you can to talk him into it. Without getting too blatant about it, put it to him that he owes me a favor. Okay?"

"No."

"Huh?"

"I said no. Nothing doing." Her jaw was set defiantly.

"What the hell is this?"

"I wouldn't lift a finger for that miserable bastard."

"What miserable bastard?" I was absolutely confounded.

"Lonnie Raintree. Anyone who can use a woman that way and doesn't have the balls to do the honorable thing deserves to rot in prison."

"For crying out loud, Trish, this is no time for a feminist position paper. Besides, Lonnie is going to do the honorable thing."

"That's not honor, that's expedience. He's just getting tired of prison. And have you once thought of what this is going to do to poor Bonnie?"

Trish fumed and Roy chuckled. "You got a live one here, Dave."

"Up yours, you smirking sonofabitch," Trish snapped at Roy. "You're both so goddam insensitive you belong in a cell with Lonnie."

Roy frowned and got to his feet. "I think I'll find me an all-male bar. Dave, I'll take care of those calls. You'd better take care of Gloria Steinem over here." He shuffled to the door, paused, and said over his shoulder, "Don't forget, pal—you owe me a story."

I turned back to Trish and looked at her for a long minute, shaking my head. "The fact is, the girl was a tramp, Trish. No fair blaming Lonnie and his buddies. They were lured."

That seemed to take a little wind out of her sails. "You didn't say that. You made it sound like they raped her. 'Gang-bang!' What a disgusting term!"

I was on the verge of following up with some soothing comments when the phone rang. I picked it up. It was Dennis. "I'm with Pinky Ryan," he blurted. "Fiona just called. She's in Miami."

"Miami? Is she all right?"

"I don't know, she didn't say. She just told her father to get in touch with you as soon as possible. She wants you to call her." He gave me a number with a 305 prefix. "I'll stand by."

"Right." I dialed the number. The phone rang half a count and someone picked up. A quiet, nondescript voice uttered a monosyllabic "Yes?"

"Fiona?"

"Who's this?"

"Fiona, that is you."

"Dave! Thank God."

"Where the hell are you? Are you all right?"

"Yes. So far, anyway."

"What's going on? What happened to you? Where'd you disappear to? I've been worried silly."

"I've found. . . um, the man you're looking for," she said. Her cautious phrasing told me she wasn't alone.

"The guy with one eye?"

"Yes."

"How'd you find him?"

"He found me. He called me two days ago."

"Who? What's his name? Do I know him?"

"No, but I do. His name is Rudy Hitzing and he works for Mark Fioretta."

"So I was right."

"You'd guessed?"

"Yes. Why'd he contact you, this Hitzing?"

"He's right here. He can explain it himself."

"How come you asked your father to bring me in? I thought you wanted to settle this privately."

"I'm scared, Dave. This thing has gotten out of hand. And I miss you."

I opened my mouth for a protestation of love but Trish's hard stare inhibited me. I'd suffered one liberationist harangue and the prospect of another on the theme of man's false-heartedness appealed to me not at all. I simply said, "Ditto here."

"I'll turn you over to Hitzing."

"Bolt?" Hitzing's voice was low and nasal and feeble and sounded as if even that one word was a major ordeal.

"Who you workin' for?"

"The Commissioner of Baseball," I said.

"What kind of a deal can you make me? Fiona said you wouldn't fuck me around."

"What kind of deal do you want? Fiona hasn't told me anything."

"I want pertection."

"Who from?"

"Fioretta."

"You better start from the beginning, pal."

He debated a long minute. "You fuck me around, I'll slit her throat."

"Go ahead, Hitzing. Talk."

His weak, faltering voice picked up strength as he narrated his story. "I guess you know I was one of the guys who took care of Willie Hesketh. I guess you also know that while we was punching him out, he got a piece of me. Got me good in the eye, to be exack. So afterwards, my partners took me to this croaker in St. Augustine, a friend of Mr. Fioretta's who happens to owe him some favors."

"Go on."

"This croaker, he does what he can, but he can't save my eye. When I wake up, I'm in kind of a recovery room in this guy's office, see. My head is killing me, I mean it feels like a Greyhound bus run over it. But still, my mind is functioning pretty good. And it occurs to me. I got a little problem."

I began to visualize it. "Which is that your life is in danger."

"Exackly. When Willie Hesketh wakes up—which is why I was in favor of snuffing him, not just busting him up—he's gonna tell everybody he poked my eye out, right? Now the whole world's gonna be lookin' for a guy walkin' around wit' one eye. And when they find me, then they got Mr. Fioretta, you follow me?"

"I follow you."

"Okay, so I'm layin' there figuring any minute now one of my partners is gonna walk in and dispatch me, if you get what I mean. So I climb out of this window and make my way to US 1. And I come to this motel. I find an unlocked car and jump it and drive it to Miami. My wife's folks own this little vacation house on Northwest 79th Street, not far from Hialeah. That's where I am now. And I figure it ain't long before my pals figure that out."

I got the exact address out of him. "Why did you call Fiona?"

"Whaddayou, a schmuck? Who else is gonna perteck me? I might of gone to the FBI, but the radio says they haven't even been called into the case yet on account of nobody can figure out if an interstate crime has been committed. In fack, the guy on the radio says nobody can even figure out if any crime has been committed at all. I can't figure that one out. Anyways, all I know is, my body's in big demand and I want to get to Fioretta before he gets to me. Now, can you help me or not?"

"You got it. Sit tight. Somebody'll be there within a couple of hours. Let me speak to Fiona again."

"Just make it snappy, chappy."

"Fiona?"

"I'm here."

"Does your father employ any, uh. . ." I sought a delicate phrase for it.

"A goon squad? I told you, Dave, that's never been his way. But he does employ some very large men for what he calls defensive purposes." There was a shadow of laughter in her voice that filled me with longing.

"All right, we'll give your father a chance to settle his private quarrel with Mark Fioretta. I'm dispatching help as soon as I hang up. You'll have it on the next plane out of Pittsburgh."

"And you?" she breathed. "When will I have you?"

"I'll be down tomorrow first thing."

"Godspeed, darling."

I cut the call off, kept my finger on the button a moment, then dialed Pinky Ryan. Dennis picked up on an extension.

"Mr. Ryan, we've got one of the guys who beat up Willie and Fiona is with him. Fioretta's men are descending on him and we need reinforcements. Fiona says you might be able to assemble a little contingent."

"Yes, certainly."

"Can I play, too?" my irrepressible assistant interjected.

"The more the merrier. I want half a dozen people on the next plane to Miami. I'll give you an address. They'll need firearms but make sure they don't carry them on their persons—put them all in a suitcase or something or they'll be stopped at the security gate."

"Right."

"When you get down there, form some kind of defense perimeter until I arrive. If the enemy gets there first, start the war without me. But no gunplay if you can help it. I don't want police. That'll make it more public than a State of the Union address."

I hung up and looked at Trish. "Look, can we suspend the vaginal politics for a while? I want you to call the commissioner right away. He has Mark Fioretta under surveillance. Tell him not to be surprised if Fioretta suddenly decides to hop a plane to Miami."

"And if Fioretta does?"

"Tell the commissioner to let him. Then talk to him about Lonnie Raintree."

"I'm still not happy about that."

"I don't pay you to be happy."

She jumped up and kissed me. "Ah, now you're the same big prick I've adored from afar for all these many years."

Chapter XIV

$\bullet\ \bullet\ \bullet\ \bullet$

The driver started to turn into Northwest 78th Street but I told him to let me off on the corner at Northwest 27th Avenue, I'd walk the rest of the way. I stepped out of the taxi into the pleasant late-afternoon warmth of Miami in March. I knew there must be a breeze, the palms along 27th Avenue had swayed like hula dancers. But no breath penetrated to the quiet residential street and moments after the air-conditioned taxi pulled away, I felt sweat trickling down my underarms. The street was all but devoid of people. An elderly man sudsed his car in his driveway and a plump woman in garish slacks and blouse was nipping rosebuds on a rustic fence. Wouldn't they be surprised to see all-out war erupt in front of the blue stucco house four or five doors down!

I realized, as I approached that house that, with typical obtuseness, I had not considered until this moment the possibility that Fioretta's men had not only discovered their errant companion's whereabouts but had gotten to him before Dennis and the Ryan contingent could. For all I knew, I was about to be received by a welcoming committee of distinctly hostile stripe.

Little wonder my pace slowed as I neared the boundary line of the property. I tuned my eyes and ears to receive vibrations from the two-story cottage hunkered behind a tiny patch of unkempt lawn guarded by a low scruffy hedge interwoven with honeysuckle vines. A plastic flamingo stood like a ridiculous sentinel beside a slate path.

The upper windows of the house reflected the setting sun and offered no clue as to the character of the person or persons observing me through them. I knew only that I was being watched. I quickly reviewed my life and raison d'être and—except for Fiona—failed to find too many good reasons why I should not pivot on my heels that moment, catch a taxi for Miami Beach and spend a well-earned holiday on the strand at the Doral or Fontainebleau. This whole adventure from beginning to end had been activated by other people. I'd have been perfectly content to sit by watching the owners and players destroy each other which would hopefully restore a modicum of reason and humility to the two parties to say nothing of restoring, when the dust settled, the fan to his proper place as the true reigning deity of the sports world. Instead, I was, possibly, on the verge of submitting my skull and torso to the crossfire of people I'd never seen or heard of a scant twenty-four hours ago, people I couldn't care less about except that they'd ruined the life of a client of mine who shouldn't have stuck his neck out, to begin with.

As I turned into the slate walk leading to the house, I decided that if I survived this number, I'd have to take the good Lord aside for a serious chat about His notions of justice.

"Bang Bang, You're Dead!"

The blessedly familiar voice seemed to come from the elevated porch but the two wooden beach chairs were unoccupied. Then I noticed a snatch of blue linen protruding from behind the whitewashed wooden pillar supporting the second-floor porch.

"You'd better tuck your shirttails in before Fioretta's people arrive, Dennis." It was a miracle he'd concealed so much of himself behind that column, but the ex-basketball player was all height and no width.

He jumped down and pounced beside me like a cat. "No sign of our turkeys," he grinned.

"Good." I followed him through the screen door and immediately found myself gazing into the twin blue muzzles of a shotgun. It was trained on me by an oak tree of a black man, at least two hundred and seventy pounds of prime lean beef supporting a shaved head the color and, I suspected, density of ebony. "Why isn't this man rushing for the Steelers?" I laughed nervously at Dennis, nudging the weapon aside with the back of my hand after Dennis signaled the man that I was one of the good guys. Dennis smiled but this monolith glared at me humorlessly and took up his post again at the front door.

We stepped out of the hallway into a bright living room furnished in simple cheap Danish Modern, predominantly pink foam rubber sofas and chairs resting on a floral-pattern linoleum carpet on which lay two or three small purple throw rugs. Heavy, nubby, purple curtains filtered out some of the direct sunlight but it poured in through the gaps where two more of Pinky Ryan's ruffians stood peering into the street. They weren't quite as big as the cat who had greeted me at the door but they possessed a comforting bulk. They also wielded comforting-looking firearms, one a long-barreled .38 revolver, the other a foreign-looking hunting rifle that looked capable of bringing down beasts the size of Macy's Thanksgiving Day Parade floats.

I looked at the mantel of a false fireplace. Fiona and her father stood at either side. Ryan looked wan and apprehensive, Fiona self-conscious, a crimson tinge on her cheeks reflecting, I reckoned, her happiness to see me mingled with compunction about displaying it publicly. She was dressed in a wine-colored cashmere skirt and sweater, winter garb obviously thrown on in her haste to get down to Florida from Pittsburgh. In fact, nobody in the room was dressed for warm weather and it smelled faintly of sour perspiration.

I crossed the room and took Fiona's hand. "I'm glad you're all right."

She squeezed my hand and smiled. "Thank God you're here." There was something cryptic in the way she pronounced her greeting, something that went beyond personal gratification over seeing me. Her lips were glad but her eyes were troubled. I didn't understand, and a subtle shake of her head warned me not to ask now.

I looked at her father, trying to grasp what was wrong. Had I interpreted the strange, otherworldly look in his eyes properly, I could have averted the awful scene that was to come. But I took it to mean only fatigue. He stared at the front door, standing motionlessly like one of those deranged seaport fathers who gaze endlessly at the horizon waiting for their drowned sons to return to port. He was immaculately attired in his three-piece serge suit but didn't appear discomfited by the heat, though his brow was beaded with droplets of sweat. His arms were crossed, and his right hand clutched an army-issue .45 automatic. As boots at Fort Sam Houston, we'd been taught that the breeze from a near-miss fired by that weapon was invariably fatal.

Ryan's sphinxlike pose lasted only a moment. Then he blinked and recognition came back into his eyes. "Ah, Dave!"

"No sign of Fioretta's troops, I gather?"

"No, not yet."

"How many are we altogether?"

Ryan did a silent calculation. "Well, there's you and your sidekick, who incidentally—"

I held up my hands. "No time for complaints now, Mr. Ryan."

"Very well. Anyway, there's Fiona and myself, my three men down here, and two more upstairs. Now all we need is an enemy."

"They're only a phone call away," I said.

"Fioretta, too?"

"Yes. I think I can get him down here, too."

"Good. I want Fioretta." That unearthly gleam returned to his eyes momentarily, like a solar flare leaping off the sun's corona.

Again I mistook that look for something less ominous and I merely replied, "So do I. Now, where's this Hitzing?"

"We've got him upstairs. He's being comforted by two more of Pinky's people," Dennis said.

"Can you have him brought down?"

Ryan gestured at a stumpy, swarthy, black-bearded man in a turtleneck sweater, who was one of the two men posted at the living room windows. He walked past me and trotted up a stairway just outside the living room. A moment later I heard the thumps of multiple footsteps on the stairs and Ryan's lieutenant re-entered the room shoving a tall, unshaven wreck of a man before him. Hitzing still wore the dark pants and shirt he must have had on when he grappled with Willie but they were dusty and bloodstained and both pants and shirts had rents in them through which his sallow flesh winked obscenely. He wore a fresh bandage over his left eye, probably Fiona's contribution, but his cheeks and chin carried a week of salt-and-pepper stubble that blended with graying black hair. His head tilted as we addressed him as if the loss of sight in one eye had also affected his hearing. I tried to work up a hatred for the man but he was just too damn pathetic.

"Hitzing, I want you to call your Mr. Fioretta."

I can't really say he raised his eyebrows since I couldn't see both of them but he did raise one of them. "What do you want me to tell him?"

"Tell him you're hiding out and you want to make a deal with him."

"What kind of deal?"

"You don't want to discuss it over the phone. You've got to see him personally. Tell him you've sent a signed confession to an attorney friend of yours and if anything happens to you, he's to open it and act accordingly."

"Not bad. Why didn't I think of that?"

"Because you're a stupid bastard. But we've known that all along. You know Fioretta's number?"

"Yeah."

"Call it. Tell him to come down on the next plane. Give him this address."

"You'll perteck me?"

"Does it make you nervous not to know?"

"Of course it does."

"Good."

Chapter XV

• • • •

"Okay, everybody," I crooned through a megaphone made out of a rolled-up magazine, "take your places for the Head-Knocking Scene."

It was eight-thirty. Mark Fioretta had told Hitzing he'd catch the six-thirty flight out of Pittsburgh, arriving in Miami at approximately eight-thirty. The airport was only some ten minutes away and a phone call to Eastern's Flight Information established that the plane had just landed.

Fioretta would, undoubtedly, have called his yeggs down in Florida, Hitzing's former accomplices who were riding around looking for Hitzing and instructed them to meet him when he deplaned. That meant at least three men plus Fioretta, more if Fioretta brought some of his enforcers with him on the plane. Those were reasonable odds. All things being even, the advantage belonged to us, the defenders, especially if Fioretta expected to find only Hitzing.

The time since Hitzing's phone call had passed quickly enough. Dennis had trotted out to a grocery, picked up some steaks, potatoes, and beer, and cooked us up a wingding of a meal and we'd passed the remaining time trading dirty jokes.

I'd tried to isolate Fiona to talk to her, to say a few intimate things, but she never left her father's side, and toward the end of the meal, the two absented themselves from our felicity. They went upstairs and we could hear their murmurs from time to time, occasionally breaking into angry jabs of sound. They were quarreling about something, and whatever it was, they'd better resolve it before the big production number.

At that point, Dennis said, "I'm nervous about Ryan."

"Why?"

"He's acting creepy-like."

"I noticed the same thing. What do you think it means?"

"He's planning something that ain't in the script."

"You think that's what they're quarreling about upstairs?"

"Possibly."

"Well," I said, thinking but drawing a blank, "keep an eye on him. What've you got for a weapon?"

"This." He reached into his pants pocket and pulled out a .22 revolver. His enormous hand, which I'd seen clutch a basketball the way some people clutch a softball, dwarfed it and made it look like a water pistol.

"What do you expect to do with that?" I laughed.

"Would you like me to fire it once into your ear?"

"No. But it reminds me, I don't have a weapon myself."

I was considering a remedy for this oversight when one of Ryan's minions tapped his watch crystal, indicating it was time to set up the ambush. That's when I started making like Busby Berkley with a megaphone.

Ryan and Fiona marched heavily downstairs, the father looking haggard and uptight and slightly ridiculous wagging that enormous .45 around in his thin, delicate hand, the daughter looking skittish and guilty. A silvery glint in her hand drew me to a chrome-plated, pearl-handled small-caliber automatic. "Pistol-packin' mama," I chided her but she smiled abstractedly and walked past me into the living room. Hitzing was dozing on one of the sofas. She tapped his shin with the barrel of the gun and he woke with a snorting start, clutching his bandage.

When everybody was assembled in the living room, I went over the plan again. There were nine of us, not counting Hitzing, our Judas goat. We would station three men across the street, two in the backyard, and four in the house. With luck and finesse, we'd be able to pick off Fioretta's pawns without firing a shot as they divided to cover the front and rear doors. One of their men would probably remain at the wheel of the car, and he ought to make easy pickings. Fioretta himself and the one or two bodyguards accompanying could probably be rushed successfully if Hitzing played his role convincingly.

George Balanchine had never choreographed a ballet better and I was feeling rather smug about our chances of success when Ryan raised his .45 and pressed it to Dennis's skull. "If you stay perfectly still, I'll permit you to carry your head back to New York," he said. He gestured at the Otis Sistrunk type. "Please remove this gentleman's gun. It's in his right-hand pants pocket."

I surged forward a step. "Ryan, what the hell do you think you're doing?"

"No further, Bolt, if you please. I really don't want to hurt your friend, even though I owe him a considerable debt for the way he manhandled me. Mr. Pritzker, would you please frisk Mr. Bolt for weapons?"

Another of Ryan's bulldozers, the one with a black wiry beard who looked like an economy-sized Sikh assassin, ran his hands expertly over my bod and shrugged.

"I'll take over the running of this operation now, Bolt, if you don't mind."

"You're gonna do something awful foolish, Mr. Ryan," I said. "The keynote of my mission has been discretion but you're gonna blow this thing right onto page one and probably draw us all juicy prison terms."

"I don't think so," he said, and there went that dreamy, glazed smile I'd been wondering about all night. The man, I realized—realized too late—had become unglued. "Fiona, if you will, please."

I looked at Fiona. She was training that nifty little pistol on my groin. That her hand was shaking was small comfort: at that range, it simply meant that a shot aimed at my left kidney would hit my right one. "Fiona," I said with the disappointed tone of a father remonstrating with a child who's crayoned the playroom wall, "you're not really gonna go through with this."

She looked at me with guilt in her eyes but not enough of it. There was enough grim resignation along with it to make me hesitate about doing something rash. "Please, Dave, don't give me a hard time," she said apologetically.

I looked over at Dennis and he shrugged stoically.

"Take them upstairs," Ryan commanded his daughter.

Dennis crossed the room to the stairs and I followed, succeeded at a safe distance by Fiona. She instructed us to enter the master bedroom just off the top of the stairs. I thought of some heroic things to do, things I'd seen in the movies like slamming the door on her hand as I entered the room but it's a lot easier watching Jimmy Cagney do it than doing it yourself, and unless you've ever been in the position I now found myself in, you really shouldn't knock me for chicken-heartedness.

"You two sit on the bed, I'll sit here," she said, lowering herself into a little chair next to a vanity table as Dennis and I sat down on a blue taffeta bedspread. I gazed at the woman

I'd made love to for a night and tried to broadcast silently something of the tenderness I'd felt for her then. Her eyes avoided my gaze but only as far as my breastbone, on which the diminutive but deadly aperture of her pistol was focused.

"Fiona," I said, "I don't know if you've read up on your law but murder is a capital crime in Dade County, same as it is in most other places."

"My father's not going to murder them. I talked him out of that."

"I'm not sure I want to hear what he settled for," Dennis said.

"I'm not sure you want to, either," she said.

I pounded my knee. "I should have realized." I turned to Dennis. "And you warned me, too." I returned to Fiona. She shook a cigarette out of a box with her left hand, put it in her mouth, doubled a match over in its pack, and after a few futile scrapes with her thumb, managed to strike up a light. "Fiona," I reasoned, "I know your father's gotten the dirty end of the stick—"

"Dirty end of the stick? Dave, his life's dream has been destroyed!"

"Yes, and do you know what? He's flipped!" I answered. "He's out of his mind down there, do you realize that?"

"Dave, please, I don't want to hear about it."

"Fiona—"

Someone barked an order from the foot of the stairs and Fiona put the gun barrel to her lips signaling for silence. There was a rustling and thumping as Ryan and his Magnificent Five positioned themselves around the house and its grounds.

About five minutes passed, filled with nothing but the chirp of crickets and toads and the squeak of taffeta under our asses as we shifted from buttock to buttock waiting for something to happen. I thought I heard the thrum of a car motor, possibly Fioretta making a pass in front of the house. Then several minutes more before the ordinary sounds of night were punctuated by an unnatural thud that appeared to come from around the back door. It was not difficult to interpret it.

Another stretch of uneventful time, then the doorbell shattered the quietude. Fiona leaped off her chair as if jolted with a live wire and sidled to the partially opened bedroom door. Dennis and I cocked our heads and heard the clicking of a lock and the throwing of a chain bolt. An exchange of murmurs, Hitzing's voice a nervous croak— which was no act—Fioretta's a husky drone.

Fiona brandished the pistol at us, motioning for us to get in the walk-in closet behind some mothball-reeking suits and dresses. I looked at her and said, "Can I make one phone call?"

"Don't be silly. To whom?"

"To my insurance agent. I want to make sure my next of kin receive my benefits promptly."

She knitted her eyebrows.

"Fiona, those people are pros. If you think they're not going to look in closets. . ."

"There's a little hideout behind the closet wall. Hitzing told me he built a number of them in the house as caches for loot. There should be a little latch. . ." She pushed some hangers aside. "There." She pushed an almost invisible bolt at the top left-hand corner of the back wall and a tiny plasterboard door squeaked open. "My father and his men will be in similar ones in the other bedrooms," she said as we stepped into an airless cubbyhole slightly larger than a shower stall and made smaller by a little trove of portable televisions, hi-fi equipment, several dozen cartons of cigarettes, and four or five fur coats. Fiona slid the closet door shut, replaced the hanging garments in front of the false wall, and pulled the chain on a dim red overhead light. Then she closed the little door, squishing the three of us together in a way that would have made sardines uncomfortable.

We held our breath as one of Fioretta's men padded up the stairs and checked out the room. After a moment I heard the closet door slide open and hangers rasping on their metal bar. Then the man's footsteps left the room. We heard him call to a confederate and the two returned with heavy footsteps down the stairs. After a moment Fiona opened the door and we burrowed through the clothing and out of the closet. We tiptoed to the bedroom door and listened. A conversation between Fioretta and Hitzing was in progress. We caught only every third word, but the mere fact that they were conducting a dialogue, when Fioretta could easily have had Hitzing's throat cut, indicated that Fioretta was preparing to make a deal with him.

In any event, he and his pals were off guard, which is all we'd wanted. After about ten minutes of back-and-forth, Ryan and his bravos literally came out of the woodwork and made their move. There was a shout, followed by a shriek, a grunt, a rush of splintering crashes, and the scuffle of men locked in turmoil. Curses, curses, and more curses. Then silence.

We waited for the decision to be announced.

I heard the front door open and Ryan call out triumphantly to his man posted outside. Then the back door, same thing. Then a lot of shuffling, punctuated by Ryan's voice: "Is that all of them?"

Another voice answering in the affirmative.

"Fiona?" It was Ryan shouting from the first floor. "We've got them! We've got all of them! Come down!"

In her haste, Fiona almost forgot us, but she quickly recovered, stepped away from the door, and gestured at us to precede her. She covered us as we passed in front of her and filed down the stairs.

The living room was an absolute shambles of shattered and overturned furniture, some of it blood-spattered. It was also as crowded as a fraternity's trophy room on pledge night. I counted five members of the loyal opposition, including Fioretta. Two were face down, unconscious on the rugs, rivulets of tacky blood tracing abstract designs down their cheeks and onto the floor. Two more kneeled, groaning and rubbing their craniums and trying to use their wobbly knees to get to their feet. Fioretta himself, surprisingly kempt and manicured and apparently unscathed, sat coolly in an armchair, shaking his wavy silver locks with self-disgust. Shivering against a wall stood Hitzing.

Ryan and his wrecking crew, not a mark on them except for a trickle of blood from the Sikh's nose, fanned around their prizes, leering triumphantly. The operation had been perfectly executed. And to all appearances, Ryan's captives were going to be, too. Ryan stood behind Fioretta, the muzzle of his immense automatic quavering an inch away from his nemesis's medulla.

Fioretta looked at Ryan over his shoulder. "Okay, Pinky, now what?"

"Now you sign a statement." There was a tremble in his voice, the suppressed excitement of a victor.

"A statement? About what?"

"About how you torpedoed my deal with the Players Association and had Willie Hesketh beaten by these bastards to make it look like I did it."

Fioretta smiled. "Pinky, I haven't the faintest idea what you're talking about."

"Your Mr. Hitzing does," Ryan replied, nodding with his chin.

Fioretta looked across the room at the Sad Sack figure with a patch over one eye. "I never saw him before in my life."

Ryan smiled, a nearly psychopathic smile that chilled my blood and even brought a quick grimace of apprehension to Fioretta's face. "I didn't think you'd say anything else," he said. He looked at the huge black brute with the shaved head. "Chester?"

"Mr. Ryan?"

"We'll start with that one," he said, pointing to a strapping, long-haired kid rubbing his head and trying to rise to his feet. Ryan looked at Fioretta. "Too bad you weren't present when your hirelings mutilated Willie Hesketh but I thought you'd like to see what you missed." Ryan stooped and picked up a short length of metal pipe he must have gotten from the basement. He handed it to Chester. "You can start with his fingers."

The kid on the floor looked up woozily as Chester stepped astride his back and flipped him over, pinning him with his knees and flattening the kid's right hand on the floor. The kid's eyes rounded with horror and he began shrieking. "Hey, what're you gonna do? What're you gonna do?" I watched, half revolted and half fascinated as Chester brought the pipe down on the kid's fingers. Fiona winced and the rest of us let out a collective gasp as the kid screamed like a soul in hell. Chester smashed the hand again, above the wrist, and the cracking of fragile bones put me in mind of a grotesque parody of a Frito commercial. I looked at Fiona. Her face was the color of a legal pad, and her eyes rolled as if she were about to faint. It was all she could do to hold her pistol on Dennis and me.

I studied Fioretta. The demonstration had affected him despite his attempt to look cool and unfazed. His cheeks had turned ashen and his hands drummed on his knees.

But what really shook him up was the look in Ryan's eyes. It was one of complete dementia. Ryan had initiated the torture to force Fioretta to sign a statement but now Ryan seemed to be enjoying it for its own sake, like a closet sadist who'd paraded all his life in the drag of a gentleman. "I believe they did something to Willie Hesketh's elbow, too," he said. "Chester, if you please?"

"Ryan, for God's sake. . ." I pleaded.

"Daddy. . ." Fiona was coming apart.

Chester, however, had left his heart in Pittsburgh, if he'd ever had one at all. He kneeled over the kid, picked his right arm up off the floor, and fulcrumming the locked elbow over his huge knee, thrust the forearm down as if it were a piece of kindling too long to fit into a stove. The kid's cries will ring in my conscience forever, and I was actually happy when he went into shock and passed out. I was just about ready to do the same.

Fioretta had broken out into a pouring sweat, his brow looking like the cold-water plumbing in a damp basement. I looked at him and said, "Don't you think you ought to go along with the man, Mr. Fioretta? It's just a matter of time before he gets around to you."

It was a tough decision—either your career is ruined or your body. Fioretta seemed for a second inclined to brazen it out but he must have figured what the hell, Ryan would beat a confession out of him anyway. "Bring me a pen and paper," he said.

The collective sigh in the room was heavy enough to blow out candles at fifty yards. We watched, transfixed, as Fioretta wrote out a statement dictated by Ryan and signed it. Ryan had Hitzing sign a statement of corroboration, then Dennis and I signed our names as witnesses. Then Ryan looked at Chester and said, "Now, Chester, you may break Mr. Fioretta's fingers. Every one of them."

"Pinky, you wouldn't!" Fioretta gasped. The rest of us babbled our objections but Ryan waved his gun around insanely threatening to shoot us all. The rest of his henchmen shifted their feet nervously, wondering where it was going to end, but nobody made a move to stop the carnage as Chester wrestled Fioretta out of his seat and went to work on him, prying each finger out of the balled fist Fioretta made and bending it back till it snapped like a twig. Fioretta whimpered and begged and screeched like a woman, but Chester simply broke each member with the complete indifference of a professional torturer and was no more affected by the cries of anguish than a butcher in an abattoir.

Suddenly, as Chester was about to get to work on Fioretta's other hand, a popgun shot rang out and Chester jumped as if stung by a large insect. He looked up and covered his meaty shoulder with one hand. Blood trickled through his fingers. I looked at Fiona. A wisp of cordite-smelling smoke trailed out of her pistol. She looked utterly horrified at what she'd done but that was lost in the larger horror, and she seemed prepared to fire again if Chester continued.

Ryan gaped. "Fiona, what do you think you're doing?" He marched around an overturned couch to her and reached for her pistol. She trained it on him and he, in self-defense, raised his own weapon on her. Dennis and I didn't even have to exchange glances as we moved automatically to intercept the two with rabbit chops to the wrists. The guns came away from their hands easily. Ryan's assistants did nothing to retaliate. They were as sick of the scene as we were.

Chapter XVI

• • • •

The commissioner flew down to Miami with a small phalanx of aides to help me set the mess in order and believe me, it wasn't easy. Thanks to Pinky Ryan's freak-out, there were more loose ends than a Navajo's loom at coffee-break time. The commissioner was still determined to keep a lid on the Hesketh affair, even though we now had the culprits dead to rights. We'd committed too many sins along the way. To haul everything into the open would be to betray the people who'd stuck their necks out to help us—and that included ourselves. As Sam Metcalf had said, the thing had the earmarks of a Watergate. And besides, the reasons for covering up Willie's "accident" were as valid today as they'd been when it happened.

But covering it up was light housekeeping compared to covering up the Siege of Miami, a task which included how to treat Pinky's victims without arousing undue attention, how to explain to the world Mark Fioretta's abrupt resignation from his union, and how to enter Pinky Ryan in a mental institution for observation and treatment while Fiona took over the running of his Federation.

The commissioner tackled these with typical energy plus some cold-blooded arm twisting and, I'm afraid, another outlay of hush money. I didn't stick around for this virtuoso performance as I had one more mission to accomplish. But apparently he pulled it off, for to this day, no one has ever connected all the links, though I'm not saying there wasn't plenty of speculation.

Before I left, I looked in on Fiona, who'd spent the rest of the night in the bedroom upstairs gazing blankly out the window trying to make sense of everything that had happened. I'd seen the same face in a small Texas town the day after a tornado leveled it.

I didn't think it the appropriate time for a Serious Discussion About Our Relationship but by morning Fiona had recovered sufficiently to pursue it. "Won't you sit down?" she said. Her voice was raspy and her sinuses were clogged from crying. Her red hair was tangled and dry, like that of an invalid coming off a long illness.

"I've got a plane to catch," I said.

She rose to embrace me and had enough energy left over from her ordeal to clutch me tightly and rake my neck with desperate nails. I put my arms around her and hugged her stiffly, patting her on the back. She pushed away and looked at me with ravaged eyes. "Is that all you have left for me?"

"I'm tired, that's all."

"Tired of me, you mean." Her arms dropped limply to her side.

"That's not true."

"Then disgusted with me."

Neither word fixed my feeling quite accurately and the one that did was too cruel. I said nothing.

"My father made me do it," she said defensively.

"I don't think you really believe that," I answered. "You had freedom of choice and you chose."

Her hands opened and closed rapidly. "Dave, surely you understand the predicament I was in."

"Yes, perfectly. Unfortunately, my understanding can't change how I felt when you pointed that pistol at me." Something had died in me as if she'd actually put a bullet through it but there was no need for me to articulate that. "I've got to catch that plane."

"Will you call me when. . .when things have settled down a little? Maybe in time. . .?"

"Maybe in time," I said. "Take care of your father. He needs you."

The commissioner drove me out to Miami International Airport. Though he had more than enough to worry about, I brought up the problem of my jailbird, Lonnie Raintree. As we picked up the Airport Expressway at its junction with Northwest 27th Avenue, I asked him if Trish had talked to him about Lonnie.

"Yes. She's quite a gal, Trish. She's worth her weight in gold, though at today's price, maybe sugar is a better standard of measure."

"I don't think sugar is quite the right metaphor for Trish," I smiled.

"She sure gave me a shitload of if's," he said, pounding the steering wheel with the heel of his hand. "If you can get the guy who framed Lonnie to step forward and confess. If you can get a prompt rehearing of Lonnie's case. If you can get an immediate pardon by the governor. If Ruby Swanson likes Lonnie and offers him a contract with the Honchos."

"All the machinery is in motion now, Commissioner and I'm going off to Brownsville to hammer at the most critical link. But what I need to know from you is, if all the ifs fall into place, will you permit the admittance into the majors of an ex-con?"

To my relief, the commissioner didn't even hesitate. "In this case, I most certainly will, for the simple reason that Lonnie will not, technically, have a criminal record. His conviction will have been reversed—stricken from the records. I just hope the kid is worth all this activity."

"Who would you say is the greatest third baseman in history?"

"Pie Traynor, though Hank Majeski's performance in 1947. . ." He shifted his gaze from the road for a second to study me. "You think Raintree's that good?"

"I never saw Traynor play and I only heard about Majeski—what was it, six or seven errors for one season?"

"Five. A .988 fielding average."

"Well, I think Lonnie Raintree has a shot at that record."

"Then I'll give you all the support I can," he promised.

Then he reached into his jacket pocket, pulled out an envelope, and handed it to me. I fingered it. "What's this?"

"A token of appreciation from the Commissioner of Baseball."

I opened the envelope and slipped a check out. "Whooboy, that's a lot of goose eggs."

"You earned every one of them."

I was about to say something humble but it didn't feel very comfortable on my tongue. I was recalling the incredible amount of energy I'd expended in an incredibly short span of time on an incredibly difficult assignment.

I grinned and said, "I couldn't agree with you more, Commissioner."

The planes got smaller and the names of the carriers hokier as I transferred first at Houston, then Corpus Christi, and finally touched down in Brownsville in a rattly Apache belonging to something called the Rio Hondo Air Taxi Service. I spent the night at the ranch house of Roy Lescade's dad and mom but forewent the pleasure of calling on Bonnie Butler, Lonnie's girl. I just couldn't face her knowing that she was the human sacrifice with which Lonnie would purchase his ticket out of prison and into the major leagues.

The following morning, I hitched a ride into Brownsville with one of Mr. Lescade's hands and hopped out of his dusty pickup in front of the Border Farm Machinery Company's sales office and garage, where Walt Willitz, the brother of the girl Lonnie Raintree—or somebody—had knocked up, was a mechanic. The tedious flight from Miami and the lazy Brownsville night had given me plenty of time to think out a strategy for today and I strode confidently into the barn-like garage looking for Walt Willitz. There was no doubt in my mind that the ox-necked, red-faced, beer-bellied guy laboring with a lug wrench over the blades of a Briscoe Ditcher was he. The arms of his grease-stained coveralls were cut off at the shoulders to permit his bulbous biceps full latitude. His hair was a wheat-colored thatch blossoming out from under a blue cap. His expression, despite the intensity of concentration, was an amiable one. The impression was quite at odds with the one of a mean sonofabitch that Lonnie Raintree had painted but I guessed there was really no con-tradiction. Good Old Boys like Walt Willitz were pleasant as skylarks till you crossed them, great ladies' men and sterling drinking companions. But do them dirty and they'd as soon stomp you to death as look at you.

"Walt Willitz?"

He looked up curiously and flashed a smile. "That's what they call me."

"Name is Dave Bolt." He gazed at me indifferently, as if I might be a customer asking him if my combine had been overhauled yet. "I'm a friend of Lonnie Raintree's," I said, casting my net.

His mouth twitched. Then he put his head down and
resumed work. "Good for you," he said into the corkscrew
blade of the ditcher.

"I have a piece of business I'd like to transact with you."

"I got no business with you I can think of."

"Might be a very good idea if you stepped behind the
garage to hear me out. A very, very good idea."

He raised his eyes and I riveted them. He tried to stare
me down but I knew his curiosity would get the better of
him. Finally he shouted over his shoulder, "Hey, Donnie,
tell Mr. Samson I'll be out back for a minute if he wants
me." He wiped his hands on a rag and started for the rear
door of the garage with cocky strides.

"You won't need that lug wrench back there," I reminded him.

He smiled artlessly. "Oh, I don't know. You can never
tell when there might be a Bolt needs fixin'."

I hoped he wasn't as handy with a wrench as he was
with a pun.

We emerged through the hangar-like double doors into
a large lot on which a small armored division of threshers,
combines, tractors, and other farm gear was arrayed, shim-
mery heat currents radiating upwards into the cloudless
Brownsville sky.

The big kid sidled between a couple of balers and I
followed cautiously, anticipating violence though I didn't
know how I'd handle it. "Okay, mister, what's up?"

"Simple, son. I want to know what I have to do to make
you confess you planted that Maryjane in Lonnie's car."

I'm certain St. Francis gazed at the animals with less
righteous innocence than Walt Willitz now gazed at me.
"Why shoot, Mr. Bolt, I haven't the faintest idea what
you're referrin' to."

"I didn't expect you to say anything else, Walt, but let me talk a minute. I'm a sports agent. I think I can get Lonnie on a major league baseball team if I can spring him from prison and clear his name. But to do that, I have to produce the individual who framed Lonnie. Now, I happen to know that's you. Hold on, I said let me talk." His healthy red complexion had turned faintly ashen, his breathing deepened, and his eyes narrowed. I glanced at his right hand, which fingered the wrench nervously. He'd opened his mouth to protest, but closed it as I overrode him. "It's been arranged with the judge who tried Lonnie that the man who steps forward—that means you—will receive only token punishment, a light fine for malicious mischief, which is a misdemeanor. I'll pay that fine for you."

His eyes reflected deep suspicion. He wasn't buying it even though it was gospel truth—Roy had done some fancy political hoss-trading to achieve the bargain. It was time to up the ante. "There's more," I said.

The kid sighed. "You're wastin' your breath."

"That's fine, I brought an extra supply with me. I can persuade Lonnie to marry your sister, to legitimize that baby of theirs. And I'll bless the nuptials with a five-thousand-dollar gift, plus another five thousand to you for your matchmaking efforts."

This sweetening of the kitty was not without effect, for Walt's eyes thoughtfully roved the sky for a moment. When they came back down to rest on mine, however, they were once more shielded by that innocent glaze. "I'll tell you sumpin', Mr. Bolt. If I was the guy what done what you say I done, I'd sure enough be tempted. But I got to tell you again, I don't know what the fuck you're talkin' 'bout. Now if you'll 'scuse me, I got a country shitload of work to finish."

He brushed past me and ambled back toward the garage.

"Suit yourself," I said, strolling behind him. "Only one more thing, Walt."

He pivoted and looked at me.

"In approximately. . ."—I looked at my watch—"two minutes, a confederate of mine will be calling the local office of the Texas Rangers to report the presence of a large quantity of opium hidden somewhere on the grounds of your house."

He froze, his grip tightening on that wrench. "What'd you say?"

"You heard me, Walt." I looked at my watch. "Make that one minute, forty-five seconds. And incidentally, the Rangers are going to find a large quantity of opium on the grounds of your house. On account of I put it there myself."

I can't say his leap was unexpected but the sheer animal ferocity of it caught me by surprise. Two strides and a lunge, the wrench a silver arc in the steel-blue sky. He was at a disadvantage because I'd wedged myself between the two balers and he had no steerageway to swing in. The wrench glanced off a fender and grazed my arm which was quite enough contact for me, thank you—the welt still glowed ruby red a month later.

My only chance was to get in close to him and I immediately smothered him before he could wrest his hand free for another crack at me. But his other hand grasped the hair on the starboard side of my scalp and yanked it for all it was worth. For a moment, I thought it wasn't going to be worth its weight in chicken feathers for pillow-stuffing but I jammed a knuckle into the sensitive nerves of his underarm, which this karate-expert friend of mine says paralyzes the hair-pulling muscles, while simultaneously I brought my left forearm hard up under his chin like Coach Landry taught us to do to rushing defensive ends. As I'd thought, Walt was musclebound, slow, and inept. With his head thrown back, I was able to press him against the oven-hot fender of the baler. He howled and started jumping like a drop of spit on a frying pan. I saw no good coming out of a fist to his rubber-hard diaphragm but a slap over his ear would ring his bell and disorient him quickly.

And it did.

I spun him around and hammerlocked his right arm until the wrench clanged to the ground.

"One minute," I said.

He wasted fifteen seconds panting. Then he said, "There's a pay phone on the side of the garage."

Two hours later I took off for Bristow to tell Lonnie Raintree he was engaged to be married to Billie-Ann Willitz.

Chapter XVII

• • • •

Ever since they outlawed gunfighting and lynching, the judicial system of Texas, once noted for its swift efficiency, has become as poky and tedious as that of every other state in the union. But between the moment I made Walt Willitz turn himself in and the moment I escorted Lonnie Raintree out of Bristow State Prison, only five days elapsed. With Commissioner Bailey pushing, Roy Lescade pulling, and Lonnie's attorney and me hustling and bustling, the review of Lonnie's case moved faster than an LP record on a 78 rpm turntable. Lonnie was all but catapulted through the prison gates and there wasn't a soul who wasn't tickled to death about it, except maybe Walt Willitz and he salved his resentment with my check for five thousand dollars.

Happiest of all, of course, was Bonnie Butler, who drove nonstop all the way from Brownsville the moment word came down from the governor's office that Lonnie was to be released forthwith that afternoon. I had a lump in my throat bigger than a crabapple as I watched the ill-fated couple embrace and kiss and shed tears of happiness. Poor Bonnie, blissfully ignorant of the ax that Lonnie must soon bring down on that pretty little neck, clung to him tighter than sweat on a mule's back and insisted on accompanying him to Lubbock for his tryout with the Omaha Honchos. I begged Lonnie to tell her about Billie-Ann soon, for the longer he delayed, the harder it would be, but he wanted to savor the few days of happiness with Bonnie, and besides, any emotional upset during the tryouts might screw up his performance.

Well, I don't know how much Bonnie helped Lonnie's performance but she sure as hell didn't hurt it. After four days, Ruby Swanson told Lonnie the starting slot at third base was his if he wanted it. This is not necessarily a tribute to Lonnie's skill, as Ruby was so hard up for infielders he'd have settled for just about anything with a prehensile thumb. But in this case, Lonnie would have beaten out just about any competition you could pit against him. I negotiated a better contract than the kid deserved, but, true to my word, I still let him go to the Honchos cheap. (That situation was rectified a year later when the contract came up for renewal, by the way.)

I left Lubbock immediately after the contract was signed, not bothering to oversee Lonnie fulfill his promise to jilt Bonnie and marry Billie-Ann. Lonnie had given me his word of honor and I knew him to be true to that word.

Once back in New York, however, I began to note with growing alarm that Lonnie did not respond to my inquiries about whether he'd cut the cord with Bonnie and tied the knot with Billie-Ann. Amidst the avalanche of work that awaited me when I returned to my office, I managed to put a phone call in every couple of days to Lonnie in Omaha during the Honchos' season-opening home stand, then on the Coast and in the South as they hit the road working their way east. At first, he answered me with vague mumbles and throat-clearings, but finally ducked my calls entirely.

I began to get sore as hell but decided to bide my time till the Honchos' road trip brought them to New York.

Meanwhile, I was subjecting Roy Lescade to a lot of vague mumbles and throat-clearings and ducked phone calls, too, as he pursued me to find out what the real story was on Willie Hesketh.

These two hare-and-hound games had their conjunction on the night of April 29th, when the Honchos were guests of the New York Mets. Close to forty thousand people turned out to see this spectacle, lured by a delicious spring evening and curiosity about the Honchos, who, after play-ing the role of doormat the previous year, were now being billed as rookie phenoms—they'd won fifteen of their first eighteen games, including sweeps of the Dodgers and Gi-ants. Perhaps the chief attraction was Lonnie Raintree, who was batting .380 (it came down later in the season but not much) and caught things in his glove that a fleet of fishing trawlers could not catch in their nets.

Roy Lescade had called that afternoon to say that if I didn't show up in the press box this evening, he would ram a stake up my ass and substitute me for a pennant on the roof of Shea Stadium. Though this was a difficult invitation to refuse, Roy threw in a more tantalizing incentive. "Also, you'll get to meet Lonnie's bride. She'll be watching the game with me. See you at a quarter to eight," and he hung up a moment before a wave of questions could spill out of my mouth.

The New York Post's press box was on the third base side and I found Roy snoozing with his feet up, his slightly bowed legs parenthesizing his Royal portable typewriter and his silver flask. His shaggy hair slurred over his eyes and ears, his beery belly swelled over his belt and his hands hung limply down to the floor. He looked like some poorly stuffed poochie-doll rejected by F.A.O. Schwarz.

I considered a variety of fiendish ways to awaken him and settled for a kick in the crook of his knees. He flailed to his feet in a cacophony of snorts.

"Wake up and piss, the world's on fire!" I shouted.

"Goddam your eyes, I'm gonna kill you, you do that one more time," he snarled. He shook himself, rubbed the sleep out of his eyes, and took a swig from his flask but punished me by not offering me any. "All right now, you ol' shit, it's showdown time," he said, pushing me into a chair. "You owe me the unadulterated God's honest noshit lowdown on the so-called auto accident suffered by your client Willie Hesketh. My Mark Cross silver pen is poised over my pad of foolscap, I have all night and the only way you'll exit this box before finishing your story is through this here window, and I'd be just as lief to drop you overboard as I would a paper airplane. So hable, baby, hable, and sigue hablando till I've got my story."

I threw up my hands. "Roy, I don't know how to tell you this, old and dear buddy, but there ain't no story."

Roy crossed his arms and tapped his foot and pretended he hadn't heard what I'd just said.

"Honest, Roy," I said.

He stepped forward and loomed over me like a wall of molten lava about to sweep me into oblivion. "Dave, I tell you true, old and dear buddies we may be, but an old and dear buddyship is about to come to an end. You promised me an exclusive—"

"I thought I had a line on who did it, but it turned out to be false," I said.

"Dave, I know you better'n I know my own pecker and I am prepared to swear by any scripture you can name that you are lying through your teeth." He was breathing heavily and not a little alcoholically and I knew he was really angry.

I didn't think my intransigence would rupture our friendship but it certainly was going to hobble it for a while. I'd made up my mind that that was the price I'd have to pay, for I had higher allegiance. I can only say, reflecting on the sacrifices Roy had made to rescue me from doom, that I'm glad not everybody is as faithless and ungrateful as I am.

"Roy," I lied, "I covered a lot of territory back in March and though I'm convinced, like everybody else, that Willie Hesketh was beaten, I've found no evidence to confirm it, Willie himself has denied it, and every lead I pursued turned out to be false. You want to print that, you can quote me direct."

He collapsed into his chair, grabbed his flask, and guzzled another mouthful of bourbon. "You're really gonna stick to that story," he half said, half asked.

"It's no story, Roy, and believe me, I'm as unhappy about it—"

"Please, Dave, spare me. The bullshit is bad enough—don't throw the crock in too. In fact, why don't you just kind of mosey the fuck out of here? I got a lot of work to do."

He turned to his typewriter and spun a yellow sheet of paper through the roller. The man was really bugged.

I went to the door of the press box, then turned back. "Hey, wasn't Billie-Ann supposed to show up here?"

"Billie-Ann?" he addressed his typewriter. "Who's Billie-Ann?"

"Billie-Ann Willitz—I mean, Billie-Ann Raintree, Lonnie's new wife."

He shrugged. "I don't know no Billy-Ann Nobody."

"You said Lonnie's bride. . .?"

"That's what I said."

"Then who. . .?"

The question was answered by a tinkle-bell laugh behind me. I whirled around and gaped. "Bonnie!"

"Hi, sweetie-pie." The blue-eyed gamine with the frizzy hair, still panting from running up the ramp to the upper deck, threw her arms around my neck and printed a big wet kiss on my cheek. "Look," she said, disengaging and waving her left hand in front of my face. Her ring finger sported a thin gold band.

"Bonnie, what the hell is this all about?"

"It's about happy endings," she chirped. "Don't you just love 'em?"

"Sure, if they're really happy."

"Buy me a hot dog and I'll explain," she said, taking my hand and tugging. I leaned back into the press box and called Roy's name but he answered me by pounding out a sentence on his machine. Oh, well, I owed him a story.

We walked down to the concession stand and Bonnie glommed down a hot dog and orange soda. I, being no devotee of stadium cuisine, stuck with a bag of peanuts.

"Lonnie told me all about Billie-Ann Willitz," my captivating little companion said between gulps. "In fact, he told me all about everything. I was pretty hurt."

"I reckon you were."

"But then I got to thinkin' it over, and I said to myself, 'Bonnie Butler, you're a big damn fool.' Here Lonnie went and served time rather than tell me something' he thought'd break my heart. Plus he really did behave toward Billie-Ann in a most honorable manner, all things considered. Sure, my vanity was hurt and all that, but leaving' aside Lonnie's. . . um. . . initial indiscretion, he showed more virtue than just about any man I can think of would do under the same circumstances. I came out of this lovin' and admirin' Lonnie more'n ever."

I shook my head. "Bonnie, you are the romantickest gal I've ever met."

"Not entirely," she said, suppressing a laugh. "Matter of fact, that wasn't the reason I finally forgave Lonnie."

"Oh?"

"Uh-uh. The reason I forgave him is. . . well, you know that New Year's Eve that Lonnie and his buddies went to bed with Billie-Ann while I was out of town?"

"Yes."

Her alabaster cheeks flushed bright orange. "Well, I kind of messed around myself up in Amarillo." She squinched her face up in a kind of what-a-bad-girl-am-I look. "Of course, it was only with one boy, not five or six."

"Bonnie Butler, I do declare!" I gasped. "And all this time I thought you were the very model of modest maidenhood." Then I squinted at her. "You didn't tell Lonnie, I trust."

"Uh-uh. He's still on the double standard. Besides, I don't ever want him to have something to hold over me."

I leaned against the counter of the concession stand, trying to absorb this staggering news. When enough of it had filtered through my brain, I said, "All right, but what about Billie-Ann?"

"Why didn't Lonnie marry her, you mean?"

"Yes."

"Well, Mr. Bolt, he did go up to see her in Goliad with the best of intentions. But when he got there. . .?"

"Yes?"

"She was already married!"

I dropped my bag of peanuts. "You're kidding!"

"Uh-uh."

"But why. . .?"

"Because she had to," Bonnie giggled.

"You mean. . .?"

"She got herself knocked up all over again," Bonnie laughed. "Mr. Bolt, that girl was trouble!"

"And you don't think you are,"

"Why, Mr. Bolt," she said, slipping her arm through mine and hugging me to her breast, "butter wouldn't melt in this li'l ol' mouth."

"Let's go watch the game," I said as the first strains of the National Anthem echoed through Shea Stadium.

A Look At: The Suicide Squad (The Pro Book Four)

Dave Bolt doesn't know what the Racers' star quarterback has to do with the game no gambler would touch, but it smells like a mighty fishy fix.

When Jimmy Quinn doesn't show for a meeting and has disappeared, Bolt suspects more than a thrown game. Quinn's books show a few shady deals, but nothing too suspicious. Now Bolt has a dead gambler on his hands, and what he wants to know is...is Quinn next on the list or a cold-blooded killer?

No one ever said the sports business was a cup of tea and Dave Bolt takes his coffee strong, bitter and black.

AVAILABLE NOVEMBER 2020

About the Author

Though Richard Curtis is best known as a leading New York literary agent, he is also author of dozens of works of fiction and nonfiction published by leading publishers, as well as numerous works of humor and award-winning satire. His plays have been performed in numerous venues and festivals in New York. He is currently writing, producing and directing The Creepery, a series of horror podcasts scheduled for launch late in 2020.

Curtis's interest in emerging media and technology led to his founding of the first commercial e-book publishing company in the English language seven years before the introduction of the Kindle and the Digital Revolution.

Curtis was the first president of the Independent Literary Agents Association and was President of the Association of Authors' Representatives in 1996 and 1997.

Early in his freelance career he conceived The Pro, featuring a sports agent sleuth and action hero (modeled after Dallas Cowboys quarterback Don Meredith). Unlike his book's hero, Curtis is not very good with his fists.